Praise for Alexa....

"McCall Smith writes with clarity, humor, and thoughtfulness."   —*The Christian Science Monitor*

"An excellent, old-fashioned storyteller."
     —*The Gazette* (Canada)

"McCall Smith allows his characters to advance the story with wit amid the simplicity of ordinary life; this is the magic of his charming storytelling talent."   —*New York Journal of Books*

"McCall Smith's assessments of fellow humans are piercing and profound."
     —*San Francisco Chronicle*

"[McCall Smith's writing] is beautifully precise and psychologically acute."
     —*The Independent* (London)

"McCall Smith's characters are well drawn and alive."   —*The Providence Journal*

"A virtuoso storyteller."   —*The Scotsman*

"Whimsical. . . . Quirky and delightful."
     —*Booklist* (starred review)

ALEXANDER McCALL SMITH

TINY TALES

Alexander McCall Smith is the author of the No. 1 Ladies' Detective Agency novels and a number of other series and stand-alone books. His works have been translated into more than forty languages and have been bestsellers throughout the world. He lives in Scotland.

alexandermccallsmith.com

TINY TALES

by

ALEXANDER
McCALL SMITH

with illustrations by

IAIN McINTOSH

ANCHOR BOOKS

A Division of Penguin Random House LLC
New York

FIRST ANCHOR BOOKS EDITION, MARCH 2022

Copyright © 2020 by Alexander McCall Smith
Illustrations copyright © 2020 by Iain McIntosh

All rights reserved. Published in the United States by Anchor Books,
a division of Penguin Random House LLC, New York, and distributed
in Canada by Penguin Random House Canada Limited, Toronto.
Originally published in hardcover in Great Britain by Polygon Books,
an imprint of Birlinn Ltd., Edinburgh, in 2020 and subsequently
in hardcover in the United States by Pantheon Books, a division
of Penguin Random House LLC, New York, in 2021.

Anchor Books and colophon are registered
trademarks of Penguin Random House LLC.

The Library of Congress has cataloged the Pantheon edition as follows:
Names: McCall Smith, Alexander, author. | McIntosh, Iain, illustrator.
Title: Tiny tales : stories of romance, ambition, kindness, and happiness /
by Alexander McCall Smith ; with illustrations by Iain McIntosh.
Description: First American edition. | New York : Pantheon Books, 2021.
Identifiers: LCCN 2020045181 (print) | LCCN 2020045182 (ebook)
Subjects: GSAFD: Short stories.
Classification: LCC PR6063.C326 T58 2021 (print) |
LCC PR6063.C326 (ebook) | DDC 823/.914—dc23
LC record available at https://lccn.loc.gov/2020045181
LC ebook record available at https://lccn.loc.gov/2020045182

Anchor Books Trade Paperback ISBN: 978-0-593-31297-1
eBook ISBN: 978-0-593-31601-6

Book design by M. Kristen Bearse

anchorbooks.com

Printed in the United States of America
10 9 8 7 6 5 4 3 2 1

This book is for Linda Stein.

CONTENTS

This book contains tales of:

TALES

of

LOVE

DESCENT

Molly wanted to do a parachute jump.

"I wouldn't if I were you," said her friend. "What's the point?"

That was a difficult question to answer. What was the point of jumping out of an aeroplane and tumbling down through the air? The deliberate courting of risk? Proving something about yourself—namely that you can jump out of an aeroplane? It was not a simple question to answer, and so Molly simply said, "I could meet somebody. You never know."

"On a parachute jump?" her friend mocked. "Meet somebody? Are you serious?"

But when she went to the parachute club, Molly met an exceedingly handsome instructor. He was known as Drop-Dead Gorgeous. This was not a good nickname for a parachutist to have, but Molly did not know about it at the time.

"All right, Molly," said Drop-Dead Gorgeous. "I'm going to strap you to me. Then we're going to jump out of the aircraft strapped together. Any questions?"

Molly tried to think of a question, but could only think of asking, *How long will it last?* She was not thinking so much of the jump, but of how long she would be strapped to the instructor.

They went up in the plane. Molly looked down at the ground below. The countryside was parcelled out in small, neat fields. Rivers were tiny veins of silver. The cars on the roads were minute beetles. The earth was so dear . . . "Comfortable?" asked Drop-Dead Gorgeous.

"Very," said Molly.

The descent took very little time. The ground seemed to come up rather fast, but the instructor landed on his feet, cushioning Molly's landing. She looked into his eyes. "That was lovely," she said.

He smiled at her. "Let's not unstrap just yet," he said. "We could go for coffee together."

He did the walking. Strapped to him in her harness, her feet did not touch the ground, but she was happy to be carried— more than happy, perhaps.

After coffee, he suggested they go for a walk. "No need to get unstrapped just yet," he said.

They spent the day together, in close proximity. At the end, he said, "You know something? I feel very close to you."

"So do I," said Molly. She was convinced that she had found the man she was looking for, and he felt the same thing, *mutatis mutandis*, of course.

"I'm going to give up jumping," he promised.

She was relieved. He thought that her relief was connected with her concerns about the danger involved in parachuting, but that was not the real reason. She did not want him to be strapped to anybody else, which was quite reasonable, in her view. At the same time, she fully understood that a key element in any successful relationship was not to be too clingy.

SISTER ANGELICA

Former nun and missionary, Austin, Texas, and Baton Rouge, Louisiana

Sister Angelica was recruited to the Order of the Little Helpers by Sister Domenica, postulant-mistress of the order and subsequently its Mother Superior. It had never occurred to Angelica Docherty that she had a vocation to be a nun, and she would never have joined had it not been for the subtle pressure applied to her by Sister Domenica when the senior nun visited the St. Agnes School for Catholic Girls just outside Austin, Texas.

"Jesus is waiting for you," Sister Domenica said to the impressionable sixteen-year-old Angelica. "But don't expect him to wait forever. Jesus is a busy executive in the corporation that is the Holy Church. He has plenty of other things to do."

The message was rubbed in with references to the consequences of not obeying a call. "There are plenty of girls— young women now," said Sister Domenica, "who regret— bitterly regret—not having responded to a vocation. Some of them, I have no doubt, are in purgatory for that very reason. I'm not sure whether they'll be getting out any time soon— who knows? These things are secrets kept in the bosom of the Lord."

Angelica succumbed to these suggestions and was in

due course admitted to the veil. She was given training as a nurse, and it was while she was in college studying nursing that she met Francesca Duval, a young woman from Baton Rouge. Francesca would cook a meal for the two of them every Friday evening, and then they would listen to the collection of Cajun LPs that Francesca had built up. This would be done by candlelight, and Francesca always had a bottle of Californian white wine that she would open for these occasions.

"Are you sure you want to go ahead with this nun business, Angie?" asked Francesca. "I mean, there's much more to life, you know."

Angelica always hesitated when answering that question. She did not want to be a nun, but she was frightened of Sister Domenica. How could she ever face the Mother Superior and tell her—to her face—that she was leaving the order? She could not do it—she just could not.

After completing her nursing training, Angelica was sent by the order to serve in a hospital in Somalia. Francesca came to see her off. They both cried.

She spent six years in Somalia, never returning once to the United States. Then she was awarded six months' leave by the order. She returned to Austin, weakened and suffering from a debilitating tropical disease from which she would take months to recover. Hearing of the condition of her friend, Francesca offered to put Angelica up in the house she owned in Canyon Creek. The order was happy to accept, as this would mean that Angelica's recuperation would not be a drain on their budget.

Slowly, Francesca nursed Angelica back to health. She

cooked nourishing meals and arranged for physical therapy. On Friday evenings they returned to their former custom of having dinner by candlelight while listening to Cajun music.

"I'd love to go back to Louisiana," said Francesca one evening. "Would you come with me?"

"For good?" asked Angelica.

Francesca nodded. "Yes," she said. "You've done your bit. You worked all those years in Kenya . . ."

"Somalia," interrupted Angelica.

"Okay, Somalia. You worked all those years without being paid. You got sick. You've made your contribution. And we'd be so happy together, listening to Cajun music down there and eating gumbo. And dancing too. I know a place where we could go dance."

"But how?"

"You write a letter to that woman—what's her name? Domenica or whatever. You write to her and say: *I quit.* That's all. *I quit.*"

Rather to Francesca's surprise, the letter was written. Three days later, Domenica arrived at the house.

"I'm Mother Superior," she said to Francesca.

"Get lost," said Francesca.

Domenica pushed her way past Francesca and charged into the living room. When she saw her, Angelica paled. "Mother . . . ," she stuttered.

She got no further. She saw Francesca creeping up behind Domenica, a heavy saucepan in her right hand. Angelica gasped, and at that moment Francesca hit their visitor over the head with the saucepan.

It did very little, if any, harm. But seeing that the senior nun had survived the attack, Angelica burst out laughing. This was too much for Domenica, who turned on her heel and stormed out of the door.

"Dearest," said Francesca, rushing to embrace Angelica. "I hate violence in all its forms, but sometimes . . ."

Angelica laughed.

They moved to Baton Rouge, where eight months later they opened a bar called Mother Superior's.

"Odd name for a bar," said the locals. "But they have some of the best live Cajun music in town. Great place."

They were very happy. Their house had a porch on which they installed two rocking chairs and a swinging sofa. The bar had a good manager, and so they did not have to go in to work every day. This left them free to read, to make lunch for their friends, and to help at a homeless shelter on the edge of town. They took on responsibility for an elderly jazz musician, C# Jones, whose sight was failing him and who lived rent-free in a small apartment by courtesy of a charitable landlord. They made soup for him and listened to his memories of playing in the Temperance Hall forty years before. One Christmas they paid for him to visit his relatives in North Carolina. He wrote to them from Raleigh saying, "I tell the folks here that the Lord sent you. They say *hi* and thank you."

Francesca cried when she read this. Angelica put her arm around her friend. "He sends each of us someone," Francesca said. "The issue is: How can you tell when it happens?"

Angelica replied, "You know. You just know."

BY POST

A middle-aged widower called Henry, who ran a small garage in Dumfries, decided that it was time for him to remarry. He found it difficult, though, to meet a suitable woman: it was easy enough to meet local women through friends or at functions, but they seemed keen to discuss dairy farming—and little else. Henry was not interested in cows.

Eventually Henry revealed his frustrations to a man called Roger, whom he met in a pub. Roger listened attentively and then, with a broad smile, said, "Well, just look at me. Go on—look at me."

Henry was not sure how to take this invitation, but the situation became clearer when Roger continued, "Do I look unhappy? I do not. Do I look as if I'm not being fed properly at home? I do not."

Roger explained that he had imported a Thai bride, and had been blissfully happy since the day she arrived. "She cooks very nicely," he said. "And she keeps the house spotless. I consider myself a lucky man."

Henry found a website where Thai women could be ordered online. He was surprised by the language used: it seemed to him that the brides were viewed as commodities. The site even referred to "your order." This struck him as completely inappropriate for such a personal transaction: it was blatant commodification, although that was not a word with which Henry was familiar.

He raised the issue with a Church of Scotland minister, whose car he serviced. He asked the minister, a sympathetic man, whether it was in any way wrong to bring somebody from Thailand in order to get married.

"It depends," said the minister. "If you and she are in love, and you wish to enter into a happy marriage, then I see nothing wrong in that. But if the lady in question is unwilling in any way, then it's a different matter." The minister looked at Henry searchingly. "My impression of you, Mr. MacPherson, is that you are a decent man. I can't imagine you would behave badly in such a matter."

The discussion with the minister went no further. Back at home, he looked at the photographs and found a lady whose appearance he liked. He paid a deposit—further evidence of commodification—and a few weeks later she arrived in a taxi at his garage.

"That woman you sent off for has arrived," said the mechanic whom he employed at the garage. "She doesn't look too bad, Henry."

Henry introduced himself. The woman smiled, but could not speak a word of English, and so nothing was said. He took her home and showed her the house. She smiled again and immediately began to clean it. Henry tried to talk to her, but she looked at him without comprehension.

After a few weeks of this, Henry found himself becoming increasingly frustrated at not being able to say anything to his new wife. Finally, he could bear it no more and he bought her a one-way air-ticket back to Bangkok. He drove her to Glasgow Airport and effectively handed her over at a check-in desk. She was confused, but the airline was helpful and took her off into the departure hall. Henry waved goodbye and drove back to Dumfries. "Oh well," he said to himself, "I did my best."

Clearing out her room, he found that she had been keeping what looked like a diary. It was written in Thai script, and he could not decipher it, but a couple of months later he met a teacher who had lived in Thailand for years and could read Thai. Henry showed him the diary and asked him to translate.

The teacher frowned as he read. "This is very moving," he said. "Listen to this: 'I am so happy in this country, which is cool and green. The people are quiet and do not push and shove like people at home. All I want to do is make this kind man happy. I want him to have the best food I can cook. I take great care with his laundry. I keep his house very clean. But he does not love me, I think, and my heart is broken. It is broken.'"

The teacher looked at Henry. "Do you want me to go on?" he asked.

Henry shook his head. He went home and thought about how we should conduct ourselves in this world. He would go to Thailand, where he would enrol on a course on the Thai language. He would find her. He would look up the Thai word for forgiveness and make sure that he could pronounce it properly.

TAKAHASHI ICHIRO,
PASSENGER-PUSHER

Yes, I am Takahashi Ichiro, and I started my working life as a passenger-pusher, an *oshiya*, as we call them in Japan. For those of you who know nothing about that—and I am never surprised to find out how little you know about the way we do things in Japan—this profession involves pushing people into carriages so that the doors can close efficiently. It is a very honourable profession—I regard myself as a sort of *samurai*, really, since if we were not there to push people into the carriages then the doors could not close and the trains would not run on time. I am always astonished when I see how the doors on other people's trains have to keep opening and closing as they are obstructed by some odd leg or arm from a passenger who has not got his entire body into the carriage on time. I find that shocking, although courtesy prevents me from criticising it too openly. We are very polite in Japan, as you may know, and we do not always express too explicitly what we are thinking so as not to give offence. All I would say is this: if you were to introduce passenger-pushers on the London Underground, then you might find that your trains were more efficient. That is all I am saying. I am not criticising your trains in any way.

You may be wondering how I became a passenger-pusher. When we are young, we have all sorts of ambitions. Ask any boy what he would like to be, and he may well reply: I would like to be a pilot, or a firefighter, or a train-driver, or something of that sort. Nowadays, of course, it is open for boys to choose many other professions, such as interior designer or hair stylist, rather than these old-fashioned male occupations. And girls, too, can choose to be engineers or excavator operators and so on. This is all to the good, as I have always believed that people should be allowed to do what they really want to do.

I was not very successful in my studies at school. It was not that I did not work hard—I did. I was always studying, my nose buried in my books, but none of it seemed to stick. And when it came to exams, I found that I could very rarely remember what I had learned, as hard as I tried. My father took me aside and said, "Are you not concentrating enough, Ichiro? I see you studying so hard, and then, when the results come out, there you are with very bad marks. It is very shameful."

I told him that I was doing my best, and I think he believed me. My father was a very understanding man, and he did not want me to be unhappy. So he suggested that I should spend less time on my books and more on building up my muscles in the gym. "If you develop a powerful physique," he said, "then you will be able to find work in a job that requires strong arms and legs."

When I left school, the first job the labour exchange sent me to was that of a general assistant at a railway station. I helped keep the station clean and performed any of the tasks that the station-master identified. He was a kind man, and I think he liked me. "There is a very special job," he said. "And

I am prepared to nominate you for it. It is the profession of passenger-pusher, and it requires strong arms and a tactful manner. You must push people politely: it is passenger-pusher, not passenger-shover."

They gave me a smart uniform, which included two pairs of white gloves. I wore the gloves on alternate days, taking a pair home each night to be laundered and pressed. I was very proud of this uniform and of my position in the station. The station-master was very proud of me too. "You will go far," he said. "Very far." I waited for him to explain, but he did not say anything more.

I had been a passenger-pusher for four years when I was approached by a woman who used to board a train at our station every day. I knew her, as I had pushed her on several occasions, and she had always smiled as I pushed her into the carriage. "You have very gentle hands," she said to me. "I do not mind being pushed by you."

This woman owned a bar in a nearby city. She asked me whether I would like to come and work for her. "I need a doorman," she said. "Sometimes we get the wrong type trying to get into my bar and I need somebody to push them away. Somebody like you, I think."

I accepted her offer. The station-master was very sad to see me go, but he said, "I always knew you would go far. I told you that, didn't I? Remember?"

I enjoyed my new job. At the end of the evening, when it was time for the bar to close, I would have a drink with my boss before I went home. "I am so glad that you came to work for me," she said.

I still saw my colleagues from the railway. There had been a number of us—passenger-pushers from different stations— who had a sort of association, a club, really. We had a secretary and a president, and we met every other month in a restaurant. There was always a lot to talk about: passengers are always doing odd things. We would also discuss salaries and leave arrangements and things of that sort, and we would write to the railway company if any of our members was treated unfairly. We were very conscious of our professional status and even had a code of conduct by which we all abided.

It had been agreed that if you retired or went to work somewhere else you were still entitled to attend the meetings of the passenger-pusher association. I looked forward to my first meeting after I had left, as I had a lot to tell my friends about my new job. I was not prepared, though, for the reaction that greeted me at that first meeting. They were polite, of course, just as one would expect passenger-pushers to be, but they were distant. They listened to me as I told them about the new job, but I could see from the look in the eyes of a number of them that they were slightly disapproving.

I asked my closest friend in the association what was wrong. He was clearly embarrassed, as we do not like to be too direct in Japan, and it is difficult to give people unwelcome news. But eventually he lowered his voice and said, "Takahashi-san, this is very awkward. Many of these people feel that it is dishonourable to do what you do. You push people *away* now; that is very different from pushing them *in*." He paused. "That is the problem, you see. It is a question of honour."

I had to admit that I had never thought of this, but now that he mentioned it, I could see how an honourable person could well feel that way.

"I have done a terrible thing," I said. "I have dishonoured my profession."

He looked away. "I did not want to tell you," he said. "I still regard you as my friend."

I thanked him. "Please tell the others that I shall remedy this very bad situation," I said.

He nodded. "I shall do that."

I spoke to my new boss. I explained that I could no longer act as a doorman who had to push unwelcome people away. She listened to me, and when I had finished she said, "I am very sorry that I have been the cause of your embarrassment. It is I who have dishonoured your profession. I should have known better."

I assured her that it was not her fault, but she said that she still wanted to set things right. I would be given the job of supervising the young women who took customers' coats and hung them up. "It is a very important job," she said. "Your salary will be adjusted upwards accordingly."

After six months, she asked me to marry her. I agreed, and now we live happily together in her mother's house. It is a large house, and there is room for everybody. We have two cats and a fish tank with tropical fish. I am not pushing people any longer, as we have employed another doorman. He is a retired sumo wrestler and so he is very good at the job.

We are very happy. I have taken up a new hobby—making kites. My kites fly well, soaring in the wind, touching the sky above my head, white squares that dip and dance, their tails streaming behind them like lines of tiny birds.

I watch my kites and think of reasons to be pleased with the world. Sometimes it seems like a very long list, sometimes it is much shorter: kites, clear skies, friends, love, the sight of a dove on a branch. You do not need much more than that, I think.

Amuse-bouche

ROMANCE

&

RELATIONSHIPS

THE BUNGEE JUMP

A young man in New Zealand loved a young woman, but was turned down.

Undeterred, he invited her to watch him bungee jump.

216 metres

At the bottom of the fall, he shouted, "I love you! Marry me!"

Touched to the core, she accepted.

yes! oh yes!

Some rebound affairs work.

PERFECT WILLIAM

William was well-built, handsome, and popular.

He was fond of listing the faults of others. His friends, it seemed to him, embodied all the vices …

Mavis, an iconoclast, found William unbearable. "Make a list of your own faults," she said … (that would teach him!)

William sat down to do this, but he soon found it defeated him …

He could not think of one – not one, and so he listed Mavis's faults instead.

Walter was terribly plain. He had been a plain boy and then a plain young man.

But he was realistic too. He pursued plain girls.

They spurned him.

So he took a chance and invited a real looker on a date ...

She accepted. She was tired of vain good-looking men. Walter was ideal in her eyes.

Aim high.

HAROLD'S DOG

Harold, a New York socialite, had everything.

His friends scratched their heads: what to give Harold for his 40th birthday? An idea ...

> A dog!

Harold liked the dog, a Portuguese Water Dog (very fashionable). He named it "Harold's Dog".

CHIEN

Friends said: how typical of his egotism! Calling the dog by his own name!

Not that it mattered to the dog.

TALES

of

POPE RON

THE FIRST ADVENTURE

of

POPE RON

Pope Ron, the first Australian pope, came from a small town south of Perth. His father, Bill Stokes, was an agricultural machinery salesman; his mother, Sandra, gave music lessons at the local high school. Ron, who had been an enthusiastic altar-boy, had nursed an ambition to be a priest, from his early days, and nobody was surprised when he enrolled in a seminary at the age of sixteen.

"God's called Ron," his mother announced in her Christmas letter to relatives. "He's called him to Melbourne to study for the priesthood. I fully believe He's planning to send him to Rome thereafter."

"We're very proud of Ron," wrote her sister in response. "Ron will take to Rome like a dog to water."

"I think you mean *duck* to water," muttered Sandra as she read the letter.

And he did. Twenty years later, Ron was appointed a bishop, and then, at the comparatively early age of forty-nine, he became a cardinal. Three years later, in an election that astonished Vatican observers, the white smoke that billowed from the Sistine Chapel chimney heralded the choosing of the first Australian pope.

But Ron was unhappy. He had grown tired of Rome, and he found the atmosphere of the Vatican, with its intrigues and back-biting, unpleasantly oppressive. He missed the open skies of Western Australia. He missed the beaches. He missed the sound that eucalyptus trees made when the wind moved through them—"Like the sound of the sea," he said.

"I miss Australia," he remarked to his secretary, an ascetic young Irish priest. "I miss it terribly."

The young Irishman smiled. "Take a holiday," he said. "You're Pope, Your Holiness. You can do whatever you like."

Ron booked a flight to Australia via Singapore. He did not want to travel in state; he wanted to be in the Economy section of the aeroplane amongst ordinary people. To this end, he did not travel in white robes, but in a beige linen suit that he had owned since his student days. It was shabby, but it was comfortable.

Unfortunately, Ron was spotted by the purser of the plane, a devout Catholic called Godfrey Hodges.

"That's the Pope back there in Row 64," he whispered to one of the flight attendants. "I'm going to bring him up to First Class. We can't have the Pope in Economy."

"Of course not," said the attendant. "I'll come with you."

They made their way to the rear of the plane.

"Your Holiness must come up to First Class," said Godfrey unctuously, as he leaned forward to address the Pope.

The Pope looked about anxiously. He hoped that none of the surrounding passengers would hear this exchange. "No thank you," he said. "I'm doing fine back here."

"No, you must," insisted Godfrey.

"Just clear off," said the Pope, becoming slightly irritated.

Godfrey frowned. He simply would not let the Pope remain in the Economy section—it was quite unacceptable. Signalling to the attendant, Godfrey then reached forward and grabbed the Pope's left arm. The attendant seized the other arm, and together they dragged the reluctant Pope out of his seat. Watching this growing commotion, several nearby passengers intervened—on the Pope's behalf. One of them shouted angrily at the cabin crew, while two others seized the Pope's legs and struggled to prevent his being dragged away. Another passenger hit the attendant with a rolled-up airline magazine, and was rewarded for his pains with a well-aimed kick to the shins from Godfrey.

It was an unequal struggle, and eventually Godfrey and the attendant managed to get the Pope up to First Class. Placed in his new, considerably more spacious seat, the Pope glowered at his tormentors. But he was reluctant to cause any further disturbance, and so he simply sat back and continued reading his copy of the *Osservatore Romano*. He turned down the First Class menu. "I shall have what the ordinary passengers are having," he said.

"But Your Holiness," protested the First Class steward. "You can't eat that stuff."

The Pope sighed. "Then I'll have nothing."

"Your choice," said the steward.

Just before they landed in Singapore, the captain came from the flight deck. He, like the purser, was a practising Catholic, and he asked the Pope to hear his confession. The Pope declined, as he said that conditions were not private enough. But he did bless the captain, and the aircraft too.

Then they landed in Singapore.

THE POPE GOES SWIMMING

Pope Ron's younger brother, Herbie Stokes, an air-conditioning engineer, came over from Wollongong to see him in Perth.

"It was a great idea for you to take a holiday," he said, as they drank a cold beer in the garden of the Pope's rented house two blocks away from Cottesloe Beach.

"I've been missing Australia," the Pope said. "Sometimes it really gets to me—it flaming well gets to me."

"I can imagine," said Herbie. "I've never been to Rome, but I think I know what it's like. All those buildings and . . . rats. Do you get many rats over there, Ron?"

The Pope shook his head. "Not that I've seen, Herb. But I've been told you get them on the edge of the Tiber—you know, that's the river that runs through Rome. Lots of rats on the banks, I've heard. And if you fall in the Tiber and swallow any of the water, you get pretty crook, I'm told."

The Pope looked sad.

"Don't look like that," said Herb, putting an arm about his brother's shoulder. "You're still Ron Stokes, you know. And I'm still your little brother." He paused. "Should we go swimming? Just like we used to?"

The Pope smiled. "That would be beaut, Herb." He frowned. "I'll have to take the Swiss Guards. I have a couple on duty—the Holy Office insisted. Security, you see."

"No probs," said Herbie.

They went off to the beach. The Pope entered the water. He raised his arms to the sky. He closed his eyes. He felt Australia all about him, and he wept. Herbie stayed by his side.

"Don't be ashamed to cry, Ron," he whispered. "We all cry sometimes."

The two Swiss Guards stood solemnly by. One of them understood; the other did not. The waves had made their blue and orange tights wet. They were dressed for the Vatican, not for Cottesloe Beach, where they were the only ones in early-sixteenth-century garb. Pope Ron was a kind pope, thought one of them, but there were limits.

YOU THE POPE?

The local priest called on Pope Ron in his rented house.
"It's a real honour having you here, Holy Father," he
said, as the Pope greeted him on the driveway.

The Pope drew him aside. "Look, Father, I'm on holiday
now. Don't bother about this Holy Father business. Call
me Ron."

The priest bit his lip. "That won't be easy . . . Ron. But
I'll try."

They sat in the garden under a large wild fig tree. The Pope's
brother, Herbie, was still there, with his wife, Esmerelda, and
they made a tray of tea for the Pope and his visitor. Esmerelda
had baked Lamington cakes, and these were served on a large
Royal Wedding commemorative plate that she had found in
the kitchen.

"I love these royal plates," she said to the Pope. "We're so
lucky to have those people."

The priest said nothing. He was Irish, and he disap-
proved of the Royal Family, but he did not want to express a
strong view in front of the Pope. After all, the Pope was an
absolute monarch, and he might be sensitive to criticism of
monarchy.

"I wondered if you could drop by our church some time,"
he said. "I know you're on holiday and all that, but just a quick
visit. Maybe sprinkle a bit of holy water about the place—that
sort of thing."

The Pope smiled. "I don't mind. As long as there's no fuss. I don't want any fuss."

"I can understand that," said the priest.

The Pope reached for a Lamington cake. "When I was a little boy, I used to love these things," he said. "My ma used to bake them and I'd pinch some from the cooling tray before she could stop me."

The priest laughed. "I hope you confessed."

"No," said the Pope. "Come to think of it, I don't think I did." He looked at the priest. "Do you confess everything?"

The priest blushed. "Well, not everything. You know how it is."

The Pope nodded. "Anyway, I'll come along next Sunday, if you like. But don't tell anybody in advance. Once I'm there, sitting in the pews, you can say something like, 'We have a visitor today—all the way from Rome.' Something like that. Keep it low-key."

"Low-key it will be," said the priest, and then added, "Thanks, Ron."

On Sunday morning, the Pope went for an early swim in the secluded pool at the back of the house. A large white dog belonging to the neighbours wandered in through a hole in the fence and watched him from the edge of the pool with baleful eyes. A few minutes later, one of the children he had heard playing in the neighbours' yard crawled through the same hole and attached a lead to the dog's collar. The Pope looked up from the water and smiled at the child, a freckle-faced boy of about eight or nine.

"Your dog?" asked the Pope.

The boy nodded. "Yup. He's called Flip."

"A good name for a dog," said the Pope.

The boy regarded him with unconcealed interest. Eventually he said, "You the Pope?"

The Pope sighed, but not loudly enough for the boy to hear. "Yes," he said. "I'm the Pope."

"Cool," said the boy. And then he said, "Okay, see you soon." And left, taking the dog with him.

The Pope lay on his back, looking up at the sky. He had been that boy, years ago. He had owned a dog called Sam, who was bitten by a brown snake and died. Did dogs have a soul? he wondered. Officially not, or so the theologians said, but how many of them had looked, really looked, into a dog's eyes? None, he suspected.

What counted, thought the Pope, was life, and the awareness that went with life. That was the precious thing, the thing against which all theories, all creeds, all understandings needed to be measured. And life brought spirit, or soul—call it what you will. It existed—it plainly existed—and upon it you could build whatever structures of belief you wished. And you had to, because if you did not, then the world we inhabited was a cavern of ice.

Later that morning, he walked to church, followed, at a discreet distance, by two Swiss Guards. Slipping into the building by a side door, he seated himself in a pew towards the back and knelt in prayer. He prayed for the freckle-faced boy; he prayed that he would be happy with his life; that he would not be bullied at school; that he would not be corrupted by the crude materialism and violence of our age; that he would have as many years of innocence as the world might today grant anybody. He prayed for the white dog, and for the man who cleaned the pool at the house and who spoke no English, whose homeland must be far away, in a place, he suspected, of suffering and conflict. He prayed that he himself might have the courage that he feared he lacked.

He sat up. A man had taken a seat beside him in the pew. This man was looking at the Swiss Guards, who were sitting directly behind him, in their distinctive uniforms, sweating from the heat.

The man turned to face him. "You're not the Pope, are you, mate?" asked the man.

The Pope lowered his eyes. He wanted to say, "No, I'm not; I'm just a boy from right here who went to a seminary and the years went by and now . . ." He nodded silently.

The man stared at him. "Can you give me a straight answer to a question?"

"I'll try."

The man lowered his voice. "Is there a God?" he asked. "In all this mess, all of this—is there a God?"

The Pope hesitated. He glanced out of the window. He saw a eucalyptus tree, its branches outlined against the sky. He saw a bird alight on the tree, and the sun was upon its plumage. The tree was God, and God was in the light behind it, and in the bird and the electric blue of its feathers.

How could he answer this man; how could he answer him truthfully, because he could not lie to him? So he said, "I hope so."

The man continued to stare at him. "You hope so?"

The Pope pointed out of the window. "Yes."

The bird flew up from the tree. Its wings were a blur of colour, and then it was gone.

THE POPE IN THE COUNTRY

Shortly after settling into his rented house in Perth, the Pope asked his secretary to purchase a car. "I don't want anything flashy," he said. "A Holden will do me fine."

The Pope's secretary was a young Irish priest, Father Martin O'Connor. He was well informed on theological matters and current affairs, but he felt less confident when it came to cars. It was not surprising, then, that he delegated the task of finding a car to one of the Swiss Guards who had accompanied the Pope to Australia. This man was the son of a mechanic in Zurich, and he had a good understanding of mechanical matters. He found a small, eight-year-old estate car that had done relatively few miles for its age. It had been involved in an accident, and there had been some body welding as a result, but it came with a clean bill of health and a six-week warranty. The Pope was pleased when he first saw the car. "I like the colour," he said to his secretary. "Well done, Martin."

"It was actually Johan," the secretary said. "He's one of the Swiss Guards—you know, the tall one with the sideburns."

"Pass on my thanks to him, then," said the Pope. And then he said, "Will he drive it for me? I've been away in Rome for so long I'm unfamiliar with driving conditions here."

"Certainly," said the secretary. Then he enquired, "Are you thinking of going somewhere, Your Holiness?"

The Pope waved in a south-westerly direction. "I've always

loved those forests down there," he said. "I love jarrah. *Eucalyptus marginata* to be precise."

Two days later the Pope set off. The Swiss Guard drove, while the Pope and Father O'Connor sat in the back seat. The Pope stared out of the window as they made their way out into the bush. "I had forgotten what this country meant to me," he said. "Can you understand that, Martin?"

The secretary nodded. "They say that everyone carries a landscape in his heart," he said. "Mine is a bit of Kerry. The Dingle Peninsula. It makes me sad just to think about it."

The Pope smiled. "I wouldn't want to work with a man who didn't love his country," he said.

After a couple of hours, the Pope's new car broke down. It was a gradual and gentle failure—a slow loss of power that led eventually to the silencing of the engine. As the last engine notes died away, they heard the screech of cockatoos in the eucalyptus trees. "Listen to that," said the Pope. "I remember that sound from when I was a boy. They used to sit on a branch outside my window. They woke me up in the morning."

The Swiss Guard looked at the engine. He tried one or two things, but he could not get the car to start. "Kaput," he said.

"It has a warranty," muttered the secretary. "That goes to show how much that was worth."

They had broken down on a little-used country road and had no alternative but to walk towards a small town that lay five miles away. The Swiss Guard found a stout branch that he made into a walking stick for the Pope, but the Pope did not need it. "I can walk as well as the next man," he said.

But you are not the next man, thought his secretary. *You are the head of the Church Universal. You are a head of state with a seat in the United Nations. You are not the next man.*

A mile or so further on, they passed a sign by the side of the road that said *Helen's Place: Bed and Breakfast, Holiday Lets. Ensuite.* "I suggest we go in there," said the Pope. "They might be able to help us with the car."

They walked up a narrow farm road carved out of the jarrah forest. They saw a snake on a bank, a thin black line with yellow bands at the head. The snake was dead. The Pope said, "Poor snake."

They continued their walk. Now they saw Helen's Place, a tin-roofed farmhouse in a large clearing. There was a barn and a small separate cottage. That, said the secretary, was probably the holiday let. "Helen will live in the farmhouse, and she must let out the cottage," he remarked.

"I think you're right," said the Pope, adding, "It would be a very peaceful place to stay, I should imagine."

Helen emerged from the farmhouse. She was a woman in her late fifties, wearing an apron. She was dusting her hands against the sides of her skirt. "You people look hot and thirsty," she said. "Come in and have some tea."

They told Helen about their breakdown. "Bad place for it to happen," she said. "But don't worry; my son is coming here in a couple of days. He'll give you a tow. He's also good with engines and may be able to fix it."

The Pope asked if they could stay until then.

"Of course," said Helen. "You can stay in one of the farmhouse rooms, Mr. . . . Mr. . . ."

On impulse, the Pope said, "Pope."

POPE RON & THE BOOK CLUB

A couple of weeks after he had returned to Perth from his trip into the country, Pope Ron was asked by one of his neighbours whether he would like to join a nearby book club.

"I don't know if you have these clubs over in Rome," said the neighbour, whose name was Bill. "Ellen and I have been in this one for a couple of years now and really enjoy it. We've got members here in Cottesloe and a few over in Peppermint Grove."

The Pope explained that he had never been in a book club. He had heard about them, of course, and he thought that a group of Carmelite nuns serving in the Vatican had started one. "Not that it was a great success," he reflected. "As you know, some of these Carmelites live in strict silence. The meetings of the book club did not involve much exchange of ideas, I'm afraid."

Bill replied that their meetings were sometime noisy affairs. "Nobody shouts, of course," he said. "But sometimes quite a few people are bursting to talk at the same time. Nobody lacks opinions in our club."

He went on to describe how the club worked. "We meet twice a month," he said. "We take it in turns to select a book that everybody then goes off and reads. You can choose anything—as long as it's still in print. We've just read Bert Facey's *A Fortunate Life*. That's a great book, Ron—all about this fellow who was brought up in rural Victoria and treated pretty badly. He served at Gallipoli, you know—survived that. Survived everything, in fact."

"I've heard of it," said Ron. "I never read it, but I've heard of it." He paused. "I'd like to join, if that's all right with the rest of you."

"That's great," said Bill. "Everybody will be pleased. We've never had a pope in the club before."

"That so?" said the Pope.

The following week, Pope Ron attended his first meeting of the book club. This took place in a large house in Peppermint Grove, where the hosts, Frank and Freda, had chosen the book for that meeting, a novel by Patrick White.

"Lots of people think they've read this book," said Frank, "but they haven't really. It's like *War and Peace.* Have you ever met anybody who's actually read it?"

The Pope laughed. He thought he might have read it a long time ago but was not entirely sure.

"There you go," said Frank.

At the end of the meeting, sandwiches were served, along with glasses of white wine from a wine estate in Margaret River owned by Freda's cousin, Tom. Then the subject arose of the choice of book for the next meeting.

"I think Ron should be offered the next slot," said Freda. "He's the Pope, you see."

That met with general agreement, and all eyes turned to Ron.

"Fair enough," said Ron.

"What book will you choose?" asked Frank. "You can choose anything—as long as we can get it at our bookstore."

Ron looked up at the ceiling. "What about the Bible," he said. He had not intended to choose that, but it was the first thing that came to mind.

There was silence. Above their heads, a slow-moving fan moved the warm air in sluggish currents, its blades casting moving shadows across the ceiling like tiny clouds.

Frank rolled his eyes. "A famous question occurs to me," he said, with a smile. "Is the Pope a Catholic?"

They all laughed, as did Ron.

"All right," said the Pope. "Let's read *A Fortunate Life.* I've read it before, but I'd like to get back to it again."

They listened.

"Because Bert Facey says, at the end," Ron continued, "that he's had a fortunate life. And when you think of what he's been through—indentured labour in Victoria as a boy, just a boy; beatings, hard, hard work—all of that. And Gallipoli, of course. And then there he is in Perth at the end, and he looks back and says, *I've had a fortunate life.* After all that! Makes one think, doesn't it?"

"Great recommendation, Ron," said Frank. "Can't wait."

"Perhaps more of us should say we've had a fortunate life," added Ron. "Whatever's happened to us, we should say that."

"True," said Frank.

POPE RON'S FRIEND

Pope Ron had spent the morning dictating letters to his secretary, Father Martin O'Connor, who was suffering from sunburn.

"You've got fair skin, Martin," the Pope said, after he noticed the younger man shifting uncomfortably in his chair. "You should use plenty of sun block—and a hat. Have I seen you walking around without a hat?" He gave his secretary a reproachful, but amused, look. "I believe I have."

Father Martin nodded miserably. "I know I should have been more careful. You forget, though, I think. You forget that you're not in County Cork any longer, and then suddenly you realise that you've caught the sun."

"Go home," said the Pope. "Go back to your flat. Apply calamine lotion to your neck and shoulders—if they're the worst affected. And stay indoors for a day or two."

"But what will you do, Holiness?" asked the secretary, pointing to the pile of letters on Ron's desk.

"We'll attend to those some other time," said the Pope. "People can't expect a reply by return when they write to the Pope, can they? Some people have been waiting for centuries . . ."

They both laughed, and for a moment Father Martin forgot about his painful sunburn.

"In the meantime," Pope Ron continued, "I'll go over

to Fremantle to see my friend Ed Birley. We were at school together. He was a great footie player."

The secretary closed his notebook. He had heard the Pope talk about Ed, but he did not know much about him. Was he a Catholic, he wondered? Some of the boys at school, the Pope had said, were not Catholics, but had been sent to the Jesuit institution because of its educational reputation.

It was as if the Pope had anticipated his question. "Ed's not a very religious man," he said. "He's a Protestant, if anything. He's a good man, though—a kind man. And that's what counts, isn't it?" He was not sure that he should be saying that as Pope, but then he remembered that he could say anything he wished.

The secretary agreed. "What does Ed do, Holiness?" he asked.

"He's a tattoo artist," the Pope said. "When he left school, he went to uni to study geology, but he didn't finish the course. He discovered he had a talent for tattooing, and he went into that. He had some sort of apprenticeship in Sydney, I think." He paused. "We lost touch. You lose touch with some of your friends, don't you? Life comes between you, so to speak."

"Life certainly takes people in different directions," the secretary said. "Look at you and Ed: you both start in the same place. Then Ed ends up as a tattooist in Fremantle and you end up . . . well, where you've ended up—as Pope."

"Very strange," said the Pope. "You know something? I would never have anticipated this. Me being Pope and so on."

"No, of course not."

"Nor wanted it," mused the Pope.

The secretary watched him. He had wondered about this

but had never had the courage to ask Ron about it directly. Had he campaigned for his election? Nobody was meant to know what went on in the conclave, but presumably discreet canvassing went on.

"I hope you believe me," said the Pope, looking hard at his secretary. "People think that when you're in a position like mine, you've clawed your way into office. But it wasn't like that at all, you know."

"Really?"

"Yes. In fact, I missed the session when I was elected. I wasn't feeling very well, you see. I had an upset stomach—quite badly upset—and I was in the men's room at the time. One of the Italian cardinals—Buonpensieri, I think it was—came rushing in to find me. He knocked on the cubicle door and told me that I had won the election and would be the next pope. That was how it happened."

The secretary struggled not to laugh.

"Oh, you can laugh if you like," the Pope said. "I laughed. I said to Buonpensieri, 'I think this must be a mistake,' but he answered no, it was not a mistake. I had been chosen."

"It can't have been very dignified," the secretary remarked.

"It wasn't, I suppose. But it was a very spiritual moment, you know. I came out and joined Buonpensieri in prayer. We knelt down, right there in the washroom and prayed that I would have the strength for the office. And then some of the other cardinals came in, saw what was happening, and they joined us on our knees. Eventually there were twenty of us there. It was very moving."

The secretary lowered his eyes, out of respect. "The Lord

is everywhere," he said. "In the men's room as much as in the Sistine Chapel. The Lord is omnipresent."

"Yes," said the Pope. "He is. And yet sometimes, we might be forgiven for thinking that he is not with us. At times, we must all feel that. I certainly have." He paused. "And there must be places where people must have felt that the Lord was absent altogether. In places where a great wrong is committed, for example. Was the Lord present in Kosovo, for example, when those poor people were set upon? Or in Cambodia, in the killing fields?

"The problem of evil," said the Pope. "One of the most difficult problems we have to face. How does the Lord permit such suffering? That question troubles so many people—stands in the way of their accepting the presence of the Lord—or even prompts them to deny his existence altogether."

The secretary was silent. It was this that had almost convinced him not to become a priest, and yet he had put to one side the doubts that it had raised in his mind. He had done that because he felt that ultimately life was not entirely governed by the head and its doubts; there was the heart to consider, and the heart was not beset by the same doubts. The heart had urged him to believe, because it was filled with love of humanity, and that, he thought, was what counted. He could live a life of intellectual detachment, governed by reason and scepticism, or he could live a life of commitment, governed by the desire to do something for others, to help them, to comfort them in their human misery. If he made up a myth to go with it, to be the accompanying narrative of his life, then what harm was there in that? That was the choice he had made, and he had not regretted it for one moment—not for one moment.

They did not explore the issue further. The secretary had his sunburn to deal with, and the Pope was going to catch a bus that would take him down to Fremantle, to see his old friend. He was looking forward to that meeting because he and Ed had been particularly close friends at school. He remembered, in particular, how as twelve-year-olds they had gone through a ceremony of blood-brotherhood, each cutting one another in the palm of the hand and allowing the resultant drops of blood to mingle in a handshake. And he had felt the need for a form of words, which did not exist, and so he had made it up—a private, home-made liturgy. *I promise to be your brother for the rest of my life. I promise to defend you at all times and to remember you when I am old.*

To remember you when I am old . . . The quaint words had remained in his mind. Well, he was not really old—not in the proper sense of the word—as he was still only in his mid fifties. But at twelve that would have been incontestably old. And here he was—remembering Ed, just as he had promised to do on that hot afternoon all those years ago.

And now he found himself standing in front of a small shop front in Fremantle, next to a store that sold Ugg boots and Driza-Bone drovers' coats. He stared at the window of Ed's tattoo parlour. It had been painted black to prevent people from gazing in—presumably people did not like to be watched as they submitted to Ed's needles. There were lights inside, though, which meant that Ed must be on the premises. His heart leapt. *I promise to be your brother for the rest of my life* . . . It was that ancient promise, uttered by one too young to understand promises, that had brought him here, after all those years. And now he and Ed would meet.

He went inside. Ed was sitting at his desk, reading a newspaper. He looked up and saw Ron. His jaw dropped, and then he said, "Christ!"

They embraced one another. Ed said, "I heard you were in town." He nodded towards the paper on his desk. "I read it in the newspaper. They had a picture of you."

"Yes, I'm here," said Ron.

"So I see," said Ed.

They let go of one another and stood for a moment in silent appraisal. Then the Pope said, "I've been looking forward to seeing you, Ed. I've never forgotten you, you know. You were the best friend I ever had."

Ed smiled. "Is that the truth?"

Ron said, "You wouldn't expect the Pope to lie, would you?"

Ed laughed. "No, I wouldn't, I suppose."

He gestured to a chair and invited his old friend to sit down. Then he switched on a kettle at the edge of his desk. "I'll make us some tea," he said. "We can talk over a cup of tea."

"Always best," said the Pope.

"You haven't changed," said Ed.

"Neither have you," said the Pope. "Do you still collect stamps?"

Ed shook his head. "My son does," he said. "I've got an eight-year-old." He reached into his pocket and took out his wallet. From this he extracted a photograph. "This is Gavin."

The Pope looked at the photograph. It was his friend, just

as he had been when they had known one another as boys. The hair was the same. The eyes. The freckles about the nose.

Pope Ron said, "This makes me sad, you know. I think about us . . . about those days. About everything that's happened, and it makes me sad."

Ed knew what he meant. "And yet, I imagine you're happy most of the time. You've got that . . . that Vatican and all the stuff inside it. Statues and so on. You get people turning out and cheering whenever you go anywhere. You've got a lot to be happy about."

"On the surface," said the Pope. "And you, Ed? Are you happy?"

Ed hesitated, but only for a moment. 'Yes, I think I am. Most of the time. I have this little business, which does well enough. I was Tattooist of the Year two years ago. That got me in the papers—not as much as you, of course, but still. And I've got Marion—she's my wife—and we have young Gavin and our daughter, Helen, who's ten. She's a very good tennis player. Really good, they say."

The Pope nodded. "That's good," he said.

"And I like my job," said Ed. "It's creative, you see. It's like being a painter."

"Like being Michelangelo?" suggested the Pope, and then laughed.

Ed smiled. He was used to people making fun of his profession; it did not bother him.

"I did a Saint Francis this morning," he said. "I did Saint Francis preaching to the birds. On this guy's shoulder. Just a small tattoo, but I like to think it will give him a lot of pleasure."

The Pope was interested. "Saint Francis?"

"Yes. I've always liked him."

The Pope closed his eyes. He saw that picture of St. Francis he knew so well, the one by Giotto. There was the saint, and there were the birds—those tiny, rather wooden-looking birds, all lined up on the ground.

He opened his eyes. Ed was looking at him quizzically.

"Will you do a Saint Francis for me?" asked Ron. "On my shoulder? Just a small one? Saint Francis and the birds?"

Ed did not reply for a few moments. Then he said, "You know, what are the odds if you're a tattooist—what are the odds of the Pope coming in and asking for a tattoo? Incalculable?"

"I mean it," said the Pope. "I would like you to do that."

Ed said, "Remember how we became blood brothers? All those years ago?"

"Yes," said Pope Ron.

"Saint Francis?" asked Ed.

"Yes," said Ron.

Ed set to work. They talked for a while but then both fell silent as the electric tattoo pen hummed. Each was wrapped up in his thoughts. Ed was thinking about how they had gone fishing together as boys. Pope Ron thought about St. Francis, and the work that kindness did in this world. Everything was stacked against it, he thought, but it continued. It never stopped. It was there. Always. In spite of everything.

Amuse-bouche

LARRY PORKER

&

HIS FRIENDS

SOCIAL MOBILITY

NEW NEIGHBOURS

Larry Porker was pleased when his noisy neighbours moved out …

He watched the removal men bringing the new neighbour's furniture …

"Anybody will be better than the last lot," Larry said.

But then …

Finest PORK BUTCHER

Sometimes what you already have is not so bad.

VEGANS

Larry Porker was a vegan ...

He regularly had coffee at a vegan café ...

But his friends sometimes let slip a hurtful remark ...

"To tell the truth, what I miss most is a bacon roll ..."

It's sometimes harder to be tactful than it is to be principled.

TALES

of

KINDNESS

JITAN

He was called Jitan, and he came from Kolkata, from a room that he shared with his father. The room was dark, the walls stained by smoke from the candles that his father placed before a small figure of Ganesh. The only window was a small one, looking out onto a wall on which a monkey sat, a chain attached to its collar.

Now he lived in a boardinghouse in a dingy area of Portsmouth. He had been a cleaner on a cruise liner that regularly sailed between Athens and Bergen. It was a towering behemoth capable of accommodating two thousand people. Jitan wore a white tunic and was responsible for cleaning cabins on one of the lower decks. He took great pride in his work and was often singled out for compliments. On his last voyage on the ship he had developed appendicitis and had been put ashore in England. The operation had gone uneventfully, but the wound had become infected, and Jitan spent two weeks poised between life and death. By the time he was discharged from hospital, his ship was in the high latitudes of Norway. The shipping company did not neglect him, though, and managed to arrange permission for him to stay in the country.

"You should find a job," said one of the shipping company's officials. "We'll take you back, of course, but you may want to work on land for a while."

"I'm very low caste," he said. "Musahar. We are rat-catchers, you know. We are very low, low people."

The official laughed. "That means nothing here. Nobody pays attention to caste in this country."

But they did, thought Jitan, just as they did in India, in spite of all the laws. And when he applied for a job in the kitchen of a large Indian restaurant he was told that the proprietor did not want him handling food. He went to another restaurant and was subjected to questioning as to where he had been born and what his parents had done. They were polite enough, but the job suddenly, and mysteriously, disappeared.

He applied to a local employment agency. He was interviewed by a man who asked him nothing about his background. After ten minutes, he was offered the job of looking after the toilets at a railway station. He accepted. The shadow of caste, he thought, is a long one.

He sent a letter to his father, who was illiterate and would have it read to him by his neighbour. "I have a very good job now," he wrote. "The pay is very good and the duties are light."

The neighbour wrote back. "Your father says he is very proud of you," she said.

With his first pay packet, Jitan bought himself a new radio, a second-hand suit, and an electric toothbrush. He was a hard worker and supplemented his wages with overtime. After three months, he bought himself a red Japanese motorbike.

There was much to do at the station toilets. They had not been decorated for some years, and Jitan decided to do something about that himself. He bought tins of paint, a folding ladder, and the necessary brushes and rollers. He completed the redecoration over the space of a weekend, working late into the night on both Saturday and Sunday.

The station manager came to see him. "You did all this yourself?" he asked.

Jitan nodded. He was concerned that he might get into trouble for acting without permission, but the station manager merely smiled and thanked him. "You've done a fine job," he said.

People began to take note. They appreciated the gleaming taps, the spotless, well-scrubbed floor. They complimented Jitan on the pot-pourri and baskets of lavender that he put out at his own expense.

"We're all very proud of what you've done," said the station manager.

The local newspaper sent a reporter to write a story on the exemplary toilets. This resulted in a full-page article in which Jitan was described as the "chief executive of the city's first destination toilets." Jitan sent a copy of the article to his father, who wrote back, through the neighbour, to say, "I am the proudest father."

One morning a policeman came into the toilet. He washed his hands briefly and then waited by the door. Jitan wondered whether he was planning to arrest somebody. But then another man came in. Jitan knew this man from his photograph in the papers. This was the prime minister.

The prime minister said to Jitan, "Very good. I read about your work in the paper. Well done. Imagine if everybody in this country took this sort of pride in their work."

Jitan beamed with pleasure.

Then the prime minister said, "Is everything all right? Is there anything you want to say to me?"

Jitan thought. He bit his lip. Then he said, "My father, sir. My father has a club foot."

The prime minister listened.

"I could look after him. I have enough money for us both. But I would like to have him here, with me, so that I can make him happy."

The prime minister nodded. "I understand," he said.

Jitan waited. The sun came in through a high window and shone on the highly polished taps. The prime minister hesitated. Then he said, "Sometimes I can help." Then he added, "Sometimes."

Jitan looked down at the floor. He closed his eyes. Had he crossed some line of which he was unaware?

Another man in a suit had appeared. The prime minister whispered something to him. The man nodded, looked at Jitan, and smiled.

EDITH VAN TWIST,
FAILED SOPRANO

Edith van Twist, the failed soprano, or mezzo-soprano, or possibly contralto—it was hard to tell—had always loved the idea of being an opera singer. As a young girl, living in South Porcupine, a suburb of the Northern Ontario town of Timmins, Edith used to pore over old copies of a magazine called *Opera Today*. She found these in the local library, where the librarian, Miss Robarts, set them aside specially for her. "*Opera Today* has no other readers in South Porcupine," said Miss Robarts to her assistant. "Only that girl Edith van Twist. She reads them all the time."

Edith loved the photographs that appeared throughout the magazine. She loved the colourful costumes in which the singers were pictured; she loved the atmospheric sets: the shabby garret of *Bohème*, the cigarette factory scene in *Carmen*, the unlikely peaks of Valhalla. She pictured herself in these settings, bringing the house down, acknowledging the ringing applause of the audience. But her reality was something different: it was South Porcupine, where nothing ever happened, where the hinterland was an endless stretch of Canadian Northland—trees, and more trees, as far as you could see, and further. Nothing ever happened in South Porcupine . . . except very occasionally, as when a boy from her class in school, Thomas Boileau, got lost in the woods in winter and lost two fingers to frostbite. Or when Old Man Anderson, a cantankerous retired gold miner, met a bear in his backyard when he was drunk and knocked the poor creature out with a piece of wood from his trailer. Or when the head of the local Royal Canadian Mounted Police detachment inadvertently shot the mayor in the foot when showing him round their new headquarters.

At the age of thirteen, Edith started singing lessons with a teacher called Violet Boileau, the aunt of the boy who had lost two fingers to frostbite. Violet taught piano and clarinet but also gave singing lessons to one or two children at the local high school. For some time, Edith was her only voice pupil, and Violet put a great deal of effort into instructing her. Unfortunately, Edith did not have a good ear and had difficulty holding a note.

"I've tried with that girl," Violet confessed to a friend. "I've tried goodness knows how hard, but I'm afraid she can't sing. She just can't."

Edith was undeterred by her lack of progress. "I'd like to go to Toronto one day," she said to Violet. "I'd like to study singing down there."

Violet stared at her. Why did some children have such a poor grasp of reality? "Are you sure, Edith?"

Edith nodded. "You know how I love opera, Mrs. Boileau."

Violet sighed. "I guess you do, Edith," she said. "But the world of opera is . . . well, it's extremely competitive, you know. Only a tiny, tiny proportion of those who want to get into it can do so."

"I suppose I just have to hope I'm one of those," said Edith, adding, brightly, "Do you think I am, Mrs. Boileau?"

Edith made her way down to Toronto at the age of nineteen. She applied for admission to several music colleges, but was turned down by all of them. At last she found a job selling programmes in an opera house. She would sit at the back of the auditorium, her programmes on a step beside her, entranced by what she saw. If only she could get her chance to join the singers onstage, if only . . .

Van Twist is not a common name, but it so happened that there was another Edith van Twist who auditioned for a role in the chorus of that particular opera company. This other Edith van Twist was a soprano who had trained in Montreal and was a member of a company there. Because she was already an established member of a professional chorus, it was decided that she did not need an audition, and she was offered the post sight unseen. Before she had the opportunity to take it up, though, she was lured to Calgary by a larger offer and the letter in which she declined the position was lost in the post. Mistaken for Edith van Twist the singer, our Edith was given a costume and admitted to the chorus.

She was delighted and took to her new role with enthusiasm. The fact that she could not sing was unnoticed in the body of the chorus, although one or two of the other singers thought they detected something not quite right. They were reluctant to rock the boat, though, and said nothing.

At a cast party a few weeks later, she met the chairman of the opera company, a wealthy Toronto businessman. He asked her to be his personal assistant, at a very generous salary, and Edith accepted. Two months later she received his offer of marriage. She decided that it was time to bring her operatic career to an end, and so she became the manager of her new husband's large hotel in downtown Toronto. She was a great success at that. It was an elegant hotel, and operatic arias played over the public address system throughout the day.

"I've had a very fortunate life," said Edith van Twist. "I've had modest talents, but I suppose I've used them well."

Sometimes she mimed to Puccini's "Un bel dì, vedremo" aria, allowing another Madame Butterfly to sing as she stood at a window on the top floor of the hotel, with the city stretching out before her, and the lake beyond it, and the air drenched in sparkling, cold sunlight, a sight as beautiful, as dramatic, as any conceived of in an opera. And her personal story, she reflected, was just as likely as any operatic plot— perhaps even more so.

MAGNUS BJORNBIRGIR,
PROGRESSIVE VIKING

Magnus Bjornbirgir was a Viking, the son of Leif Bjornbirgir, a minor chieftain who had led several highly destructive raids on the west coast of Scotland. Leif was much revered in Viking communities for his attempt to wrestle with a bear, a feat that proved unsuccessful, indeed fatal, even if it entered into Viking lore as an example of exceptional courage. Magnus had been against his father's plan to challenge the bear. "You're strong, Father," he said. "I know that. You know that. Everyone in the settlement knows that. Why do you have to try and prove it in this . . . well, this rather dangerous way. Bears are very strong themselves." He saw he was getting nowhere, and his tone became more vivid. "I'm not saying you're not as strong as this bear, but it has claws, you may have observed, and pretty vicious teeth. Bears are not pleasant creatures."

"That's why I must challenge it," said Leif. "I must deal with this bear simply because it's there. Can't you see that?"

"No," said Magnus. "Frankly, I can't."

The contest did not last long, and when it ended after a few bloody minutes, a great wailing overtook the settlement. Magnus was now in charge, and he was left with a dubious legacy, as everybody expected him to be of similar outlook to his father, some even imagining that he might himself take on the same bear, who was thought still to be lurking in the woods near Leif's settlement. Magnus declined to do what was expected of him. "I have nothing to prove," he said, and waited, his jaw set firmly, to see if anybody disagreed. Nobody did.

Privately, Magnus thought that his father had been most unwise to have done what he did. In fact, he had very little regard for Leif, whom he considered to be a typical Viking— boastful, aggressive, and constantly trying to prove a form of Nordic masculinity that he, Magnus, considered tediously one-dimensional. Things were changing, even if slowly, and Magnus was determined to give what support he could to the tender green shoots of sensitivity that he thought he detected in Viking culture.

A year after Leif's demise, on what had come to be known as Bear Day, Magnus's deputy suggested at a meeting that there should be a pillaging expedition to the North of England. "We haven't extracted any payment for some time," he said. "It's due us now. We need to don our armour and set off."

Magnus groaned inwardly. More conflict; more blood; more howls of pain and despair. It was not what he had in mind for his chieftainship. He wanted peace and, if possible, the flowering of education and the arts.

He shook his head. "I'm happy to do another trip," he said. "But let's think of doing something different. Let's seek to influence those people. Let's have them working *with* us. Let's harness their skills so that we can benefit from their ingenuity and labour."

His deputy frowned. "You mean—not kill them? Is that what you mean?"

"More or less," said Magnus. "Let's extend our influence. Let's get these people to work for us. A productive enemy is better than a dead enemy—if you can bring him on-side."

Some of the Vikings saw the force of this argument; others did not. "But we've always put people to the sword," complained one. "I would never dream of criticising our leader, but this is a bit of a change of approach."

"You have to change to survive," said Magnus. "My late father—Leif . . ."

This brought forth wails of sorrow.

"Thank you," Magnus continued. "My late father, Leif, always said: seek out the new, and then do it before the new becomes old."

"Very wise," said the deputy. "So, let's go with your idea, Magnus—whatever it is."

"To go over there in peace," said Magnus. "To go over there and offer them some sort of partnership. To go over there and bring them into the fold of our civilisation."

They loaded their boats with provisions. They took some arms, but not many: this was to be a peaceful expedition and in place of their axes and swords, they took ploughshares and fishing hooks and items of Nordic jewellery.

The crossing was a smooth one, and with favourable winds blowing them strongly westwards they were off the North-umbrian coast within five days. They were spotted from the land, where the local defences were rapidly raised. Gates were closed; shutters put on the windows; animals herded to places of safety further inland. Here and there, great fires were lit to warn others of the arrival of the marauders.

Magnus put his boat ashore on a gently sloping stony beach. Together with the rest of his band, he stepped out of the boat and looked over to the dunes behind the beach. He thought he saw movement, but decided that it was probably no more than the wind in the dune-grass.

"We should find a village somewhere over there," he said to his companions. "Let's go and have a word with them."

"Shall we take axes?" asked one of his lieutenants.

Magnus shook his head. "That would send the wrong message," he said.

They walked in a long, unkempt line over the dunes and down a path that led to a village in the distance. They had not gone far along this path when a cacophony of shouting interrupted the quiet. Rising from their concealment in the long grass, the Northumbrians swooped down upon the unarmed Vikings.

"You gave me such a fright," exclaimed Magnus. "We were just about to . . ."

The Northumbrians stopped. They looked confused.

"Don't judge everybody by the way they look," called out Magnus. "People change, you know."

The leader of the Northumbrians cleared his throat. "In that case . . . ," he said.

Above their heads a swallow dipped and turned in an invisible current of air. It could well have been a dove, but birds are no respecters of symbolism and the right moment for a particular symbol, so a swallow had to do—and did.

THE HANDBAG

He lifted up the telephone receiver, waited for the contented purr of the dial tone, and then dialled the wrong number. He did not do that deliberately, of course, nor did he do it negligently. He took just the requisite care to get the digits right, but he had misread the number he had jotted down on the pad of paper beside him. So, instead of dialling 803 at the end of the number, he dialled 808, the 3 having been mistaken for an 8. The eye looks for things and then decides what it has seen, which may be the wrong thing altogether. Most slips of that sort have few significant consequences, but Thomas's error here proved to be more significant than he could possibly have imagined when he first heard the woman's voice at the other end of the line say to him, "I think you might have the wrong number."

He said, "Are you sure?"

"Well, who do you want to speak to? I'm the only person here."

He looked at the note, and read out the number.

The mistake was identified. "Easily made," she said. "You wanted 803—I end in 808."

"I'm sorry. I usually dial carefully, but you know how it is, particularly with one of these small keypads. Our fingers are just too big."

She laughed. "Don't I know it! Mind you, it's easy to make a mistake . . . Speaking of which, a friend of mine told me about a very amusing mistake somebody made the other day. Do you mind if I tell you about it?"

"Not at all. I'm in no hurry."

She sounded pleased. "Good. So many people these days *are* in a hurry, aren't they? The older I get—I'm sixty-six, by the way—the more I like things to move at a sedate pace. I used to rush around frantically—like everybody else—no longer."

"You find time to sniff the roses?"

"That's it exactly," she said. "Some people don't even *know* they've got roses in the garden." She paused. "This mistake I heard about: it happened to a friend of a friend. He had to go to France and asked his travel agent to book him into the Hotel de Strasbourg in Paris. The agent booked him into the Hotel de Paris in Strasbourg. He was most put out."

He chuckled. "Once again, easily enough done."

She cleared her throat. "Excuse me. I've had a bit of a cough. It's lingered. I'm taking a cough syrup for it, one of those codeine-based linctuses. I don't really like it, but it suppresses the cough."

"They call that the anti-tussive effect."

She asked him whether he was a doctor, and he replied that he was. "I'm an orthopaedic surgeon. Nothing to do with coughs and colds. It's the carpentry end of medicine."

"But it must be satisfying."

"Oh, it is. Particularly when you have patients hobbling in with arthritic pain and when they leave the hospital they are pain-free. That's very satisfying indeed. Mind you, I'm not sure if I would encourage my daughter to go into medicine. It's changed quite a lot, you know. We don't have the time to spend with people."

She was interested in the daughter. "How old is she? Your daughter . . ."

"Sixteen. She'll be applying for university soon."

"To study what?"

"Medicine, she says."

"Well, that's very nice. Do you have others? Other children?"

"No. She was adopted—like me."

There was silence. Then she said, "It's good that people can talk about it now. In the past, they used to be so silent. But now . . . Even when it's painful, you're encouraged to speak about it. I'm sure that helps." She paused again, before continuing, "At least, I found it's helped me."

"Are you adopted too?"

She hesitated before replying. There was a faint hum on the line, as if the call were travelling a great distance. "No, I'm not adopted. But I gave up a child for adoption, or, rather, I . . . Well, this is rather difficult to speak about, but we seem to be being very frank with one another. In my case, I *mislaid* my baby."

He did not say anything.

Then she continued, "I left him in *a handbag*. At a railway station. Totally by mistake, I hasten to say. Somebody picked up the bag and took him away. They must have brought him up as their own."

"A handbag?" The words seemed to echo down the line, so that he heard, as through distant ether, the words *a handbag*.

"Yes. I regret it so much."

She waited for him to say something, but he did not. "Are you still there?"

"Yes, I am. Which station?"

"Edinburgh Waverley."

Silence returned. Then he said, "You're not going to believe this, but just before she died, my *mother*, my surviving parent, confessed to me that she had found me at Waverley Station. In a handbag. She said she didn't know what came over her, but she decided to keep me—and she did. She told me all that just two years ago."

She gasped. "My goodness . . . Then, then . . ."

"Then you're my mother."

"So it would seem."

He said, "You know, this story has a rather familiar ring to it. I'm sure I've heard it before—somewhere or other. A play?"

"Unlikely," she said. "But look, we mustn't waste time, we must meet."

They exchanged addresses. They did not live far from one another.

They arranged to meet. "Make sure you change your socks before you go out for our meeting," she said.

Once the call was ended, he looked up at the ceiling. Could this be true? Was she really his mother? He thought of what she had said about clean socks. That proves it, he decided. He was no longer an orphan. I have a mother, he said to himself. I have a real, flesh-and-blood mother.

He went over to the window and looked out over his garden, over the apple tree and the spreading cotoneaster. He felt strangely elated. Mother. I shall be kind to her, he said to himself—and then said it out loud.

Amuse-bouche

CHILDREN

&

THEIR PARENTS

FREUD'S MOTHER

Freud's mother was proud of her son's works.

In the street, people said, "There goes Sigmund Freud's mother!"

Then she read what he had to say about the Oedipus Complex.

INTERPRETATION OF DREAMS
BY
SIGMUND FREUD
ENGLISH EDITION

"Somewhat fanciful," said Mrs Freud. "But at least he loves his mother."

YOUNG ICARUS

Mr and Mrs Papadopoulos were interested in Greek myths. They called their son Icarus.

At the age of sixteen, Icarus built himself a hang-glider.

His parents held their breath as he soared towards the sun ...

Landing safely, Icarus said, "Not for me! I was scared stiff!"

Nominal determinism has its limits.

CEDRIC'S CHILDHOOD

One day young Cedric heard a heavenly voice say ...

Our Heritage

"Cedric, remember yours is the language of William Shakespeare!"

Cedric ran home to report this.

"Nah!" snarled his mother.

"Lol!" said his father, "William Who?"

England is not what it was.

IMAGINARY FRIENDS

As a boy, Robert had several imaginary friends.

They accompanied him to university.

Robert's girlfriend gave him an ultimatum: pay more attention to me or it's over.

Robert found an imaginary girlfriend, and went off with her.

Substance isn't everything.

TALES

of

POIGNANCY

HOUSEMATES

Jill was a student at the University of St. Andrews, an ancient university in Scotland. The university looked out over the North Sea, towards Denmark, that lay barely a few hundred miles away over cold plains of water. *Cold plains of water on which the fish are hunted* . . . She had read that line somewhere, or something like it, but could not remember who wrote it. It haunted her, as the odd line of poetry or line of a song may sometimes haunt us, triggered by an image, or the memory of an image.

She lived in a house on the edge of the town. Beyond the low wall that surrounded this house there were fields in which sheep grazed. A man came to visit these sheep each day. He had a dog called Colin, who rounded up the sheep for inspection, obediently following his master's shouted instructions.

There were five housemates altogether, and they paid their rent to the farmer for whom the man with the dog worked. The farmer's wife had cheese from the milk of a small herd of goats that she kept elsewhere on the farm. On occasion she would drop in with a gift of this cheese for the students, wrapped in a muslin cloth. "It's very good for you," she said. "Although you don't have to eat it if you don't like it. Not everybody likes goats'-milk cheese."

Apart from Jill, there were two young men and two young women. One of the young men was called Alastair. His parents owned a firm in Glasgow that made folding chairs. The other young man was called Neil. He came from the Orkney Islands, further north. His parents ran a hotel outside Stromness that largely catered for anglers. His mother had been a competitive skier who skied for Scotland until she snapped a tendon in her left knee while skiing in the Haute-Savoie.

The young women were called Angie and Georgie. They studied English Literature and Medieval History respectively. Angie came from Glasgow, and Georgie, although born in Scotland, had lived much of her life in London, where her father was an orthopaedic surgeon. Georgie had been expensively educated at a girls' boarding school in the south of England. She loved Scotland and Scottish history, especially anything to do with Mary, Queen of Scots. "It was such a pity they chopped off her head," she said, adding, "Jolly unfair."

The housemates were very happy together. They cooked meals on a rota basis. Alastair was probably the best cook in the house, although Georgie was the most inventive. "I take risks with garlic," she said.

Jill fell in love with Alastair. She woke up one morning and said to herself, "I'm in love with Alastair." That was how she knew.

Alastair, however, was in love with Neil. He said to Neil, "One day, could we go to France? My parents know somebody who has a chateau." Neil replied, "Perhaps," but he could not reciprocate the affection that Alastair felt for him. He was in love with Jill, and felt pained that she did not seem to realise how he felt about her. He was too shy to declare himself and merely hoped that she would notice.

Angie was also in love with Neil. They had once playfully shared a shower after a party, and that was the beginning of it from Angie's point of view. She thought about that moment every day, although it was never repeated, and it had been an entirely innocent encounter. When it was her turn to cook, she always gave Neil the largest portion, and served him first. He did not appear to notice this. Nor did Neil know that Angie slept with a pair of his underpants tucked under her pillow.

Georgie was in love with nobody, although she was jealous of the time that Angie spent thinking about Neil. "You're my friend," she said to her one day. "I wish you'd think a bit more about me. Neil's a lost cause, you know—he really is. You need to accept that."

Jill was fond of all her housemates. "I feel a sort of *agape* towards you," she said. "You know—that disinterred Greek love for humanity. That's what I feel. You can do what you like, and I would still have this . . . this warm feeling about you."

At the end of their student careers, they split up and went their separate ways. At their graduation, as is customary at St. Andrews, they all sang the student song "*Gaudeamus Igitur*" as the academic procession entered the hall. They knew the meaning of the Latin words, sung by so many generations of students. *Let us enjoy ourselves while we are young . . . After youth comes old age; after old age the earth will have us. Floreat academia! floreant professores! May the university flourish! May the professors flourish!*

Then they went out into the world, into the lives that lay before them.

WHAT HAPPENED THREE
YEARS LATER

It was Jill who kept the five housemates in touch. She set up the Facebook page, and it was she who posted most frequently, although all of them would occasionally send in a snippet of news or a photograph. The page was named after the house they had shared in St. Andrews, *Somerled*, an eleventh-century Scottish hero. Nobody knew why the house was called that. "We should find something more descriptive," said Jill. "But I can't think of anything—and what unites us, after all, is the house."

They kept in touch, but for one reason or another no opportunity seemed to arise for all of them to meet. Jill saw Georgie twice—once at a party following an international rugby match in Edinburgh, and on another occasion at Glasgow Airport when she was running to catch her plane to Minorca. She saw Georgie sitting near another departure gate. She could not stop, as the board had just flashed *last call* beside her flight. She called out and waved. Georgie looked up, but did not see her. Jill thought: *What if that's the last time I ever see her in this life?* The thought saddened her, and she remembered advice that somebody had given her—she could not remember who it had been—that in your dealings with people—with everybody—you should remind yourself that this might be the last time you ever saw them. If you bore that in mind, you would always be understanding, you would always be gentle in your handling of people. They might die.

Three years after their graduation, Jill sent a message to everybody to say that Neil had suggested they all should meet up in Orkney. "It would be a reunion. He tells me he has a house in Stromness that is big enough for everybody to stay in," she said. "It used to belong to his grandmother. She died last year, and Neil inherited the house and all its contents. He wants us to come in July."

The dates that Neil proposed suited everybody. "Come for a week if you can," he said. "We'll find enough to do."

Four of them arrived on the same day—a Friday. Only Alastair was late, as he had a meeting in Glasgow that prevented his arrival until late on Saturday morning. He was apologetic. "You look as if you've been here for ages," he said. "I suppose you've taken the best rooms."

But there was plenty of room in the rambling stone house that had, years earlier, before Neil's grandmother had bought it, been the manse occupied by the local Church of Scotland minister. "This is a lovely house," said Jill, as she looked out over a sloping field to the seashore. "There's the sea and there's the harbour. And there's the sky. Look at the sky. Look at it."

They looked at the sky, which was wide and northern. A flock of geese moved across it, a V-formation that was briefly reflected in the still surface of the water. "Where do you think they're going?" asked Georgie. "Is that north or south? I get mixed up in places I don't know well."

"North is always colder," said Angie. "Turn your face. If

it feels colder, then that's north. That's the way I do it." She turned round and then pointed.

"That's south," said Neil. "Look at the light. North has a blue, cold light. South is . . . south is different."

Alastair said to Neil, "What do you do here, Neil? How do you pass the time? It's so quiet."

Neil explained that he helped run his parents' hotel. "They're leaving a lot of the ordering to me. You have to order things for a hotel—all the time."

"And people come here to fish?" asked Angie. "Is that what they do?"

"They fish," said Neil. "Or they walk. People come here to look at birds."

That evening they had dinner together in the kitchen, at a large scrubbed-pine table. Jill manoeuvred her way into sitting next to Alastair. *I still love him,* she thought. *I know it's useless, but I still love him.* She asked him about what he had been doing, and he told her that his family had sold the folding-chair factory. He had found a job with a charity that looked after people who were retraining after losing their jobs. She wanted to say, *Yes, but are you happy?* But she did not. She wanted to say, *All I want is to look after you. We don't have to make it anything more than that,* but she knew that she could not say that. She did not like to think that he had found somebody, because that person was not her, and she could not bear that.

He asked her about her own job, which was teaching French in a private school in Edinburgh. There were parts of the job she liked, and parts that she did not. He asked her which was which, and she told him that the part she did not like was the self-obsessed narcissism of teenagers. "I know they can't help it," she said. "It goes with being sixteen, or whatever, but it gets pretty tedious after a while."

"Most people find a way of being happy—eventually," he said.

She did not reply to this, but thought about it. Yes, it was true. Most people found a way of being happy, but it might take them some time. She looked at him. She wanted to say, *And have you?* But that seemed to her to be intrusive. She could not imagine him being happy with another man: How could he? Did he not see that?

Angie sat next to Neil at the dinner. She told him about the PhD she was doing in Durham. It was on the sonnet form in lesser poets of the nineteenth century. "People carried on writing sonnets," she said. "They just went on and on, and they still do. There are still people who write sonnets today." She paused. "Would you believe it?"

Neil shrugged. "People do odd things," he said. Then he went on to say, "I liked some of Shakespeare's sonnets. Some of them."

Angie had had rather more wine than she was used to. It's a special occasion, she thought. Here we are together, and I'm sitting next to Neil, which is where I want to be—more than anything else in the world, I want that. She put her hand on his knee. She held her breath. He did not move it, but smiled at her.

She looked across the table, to where Georgie was sitting next to Alastair, on the other side from Jill. She whispered to Neil, "Jill's never going to let Alastair go, you know."

He followed her gaze. He said, "You never know. Alastair likes women now, I think."

"As friends?"

"Yes. But maybe more. Who knows?"

She was silent for a moment, and then she said, "Remember when we shared that shower? Remember? It was on the day that St. Andrews played Edinburgh at rugby and we came back to the house and it had rained . . ."

For a few moments she thought that he would not remember it. That would be terrible—that it could mean so much to her and so little to him. But then he said, "And we were cold. Yes, I remember."

She looked at her plate. "I've thought about that so much."

He glanced at her. "Really?"

She nodded. "Yes. *Every day.*"

He did not say anything, but took a sip of his wine. "I see."

"Does it surprise you?" she asked. "Does it surprise you that somebody should think about something like that—for years, really?"

He said, "People do that. They think about particular moments. Memories, I suppose." He paused. "I've thought about it too. Not all the time . . ."

"I didn't say I thought about it all the time," she corrected him. "I said every day. That's different. You think about things in a fleeting way. You don't necessarily think about them continuously."

The following morning, they all went for a walk to the top of a nearby hill. It was a clear day, but the wind off the sea was fresh and had north in it. They felt it ruffle their hair.

Alastair said, "What's that smell? That coconut smell?"

"That's gorse," said Neil. "It's the gorse flowers."

"Where?"

He pointed to a cluster of green bushes beside a low stone wall. "There. You see?"

They went back to the house, where Neil prepared soup for everybody. They sat in the living room. A clock ticked in the background. Jill said, "Couldn't we all move back in together? Couldn't we?"

Alastair laughed. "And stay with one another forever?"

Jill said nothing.

Angie said, "Why not? If you're with people you love, then . . . then, why move?"

THE MATHEMATICIAN

His gifts as a mathematician were spotted when he was four. His father, holding up four fingers, said to him, "Andrew, take four from seventeen. I know that's a big sum but . . ."

Before he could finish, his young son, still lisping in the accents of early childhood, had given him the answer. "Thirteen." And then had asked, quite casually, "Daddy, is snow composed of crystals?"

They arranged for him to be seen by an educational psychologist, who, when the appointment was made, warned, "Be prepared for a disappointment: many parents believe their child to be exceptionally bright. I have to bring them down to earth, you know."

But in this case, after spending an hour with Andrew in his child-friendly consulting room, he said, "Mr. and Mrs. Macmillan, I have to tell you: your four-year-old is, quite frankly, astonishingly talented. His mathematical understanding is profound—really profound. Probably that of a sixteen-year-old. Remarkable."

"We knew that," said his father, sounding matter-of-fact rather than smug. "But it's nice to have it confirmed."

They were determined to give him a normal childhood, encouraging him to do the things ordinary boys of his age did. They lived in Cambridge, Britain's great mathematical centre, and he won a scholarship to a school that offered special tuition in the subject. The head of the mathematics department said, "He's something special, this boy." He looked at him tenderly. "But he's lonely, isn't he?"

His parents knew that. They did their best to facilitate friendships, but Andrew remained solitary. Then at seventeen, when he was in his first year of mathematical studies at King's College, he became friendly with a student of land management. This young man, Hugh Holderness, came from a large farm in Norfolk, where his parents raised rare breeds of sheep. He was the temperamental opposite of Andrew, being one of the most popular and gregarious members of the college. Women liked him, for his attractive personality as much as his good looks, and he was almost always surrounded by flocks of admirers. But he was kind to Andrew, and would often include him in his social occasions.

"Odd chap, that guy," said one of Hugh's friends. "He follows you round like a dog. And you can't get him to talk about anything normal, can you? I've tried. Cricket—zilch. Girls—zero. Beer—ditto. What goes on in that head of his?"

"Mathematics," said Hugh. "He's a mathematician. That's what they're like. They're on a different planet."

When they graduated, Hugh went back to the farm in Norfolk. He did not see Andrew for over a year, but then he invited him to come up to a party he was holding to celebrate his engagement. He had met a girl called Stella, who had been working as a groom with his parents' horses. She came from Durham, where her father was a pharmacist. She was considered a bit loud, and a bit brassy too, but that was what Hugh liked. She would make a good farmer's wife, he thought.

Andrew came to the party. He watched from the edge of the room while people danced. He did not dance himself, although Stella invited him to do a waltz with her.

"I'm sorry," he said. "I'm not much good at that sort of thing."

Hugh and Stella had their first child three years later. Hugh was now running the farm, while Andrew was employed by one of the colleges as a postdoctoral research fellow. His papers on an obscure branch of mathematics were now attracting attention internationally. He had already received several prestigious prizes for his work, went to conferences in Vienna and Prague, and had been mentioned in an article in *The Times Higher Education Supplement*. He saw Hugh from time to time, mostly when Hugh came down to Cambridge to visit the outfitters where he bought his country clothing—boots and shooting jackets and the like. They would have tea together in the College Senior Common Room.

"This place gives me the creeps," said Hugh. "All this . . . I don't know what it is. Seriousness? Creaky floorboards too."

"I rather like it," said Andrew. "There are some very interesting people here. That man over there . . ." He pointed to a stooped figure drinking coffee by the window. "That man over there does work on quantum mechanics that's understood by only five people in the world. Five!"

Hugh smiled. "And how many people understand your work, Andrew? Ten?"

This brought a grave response. "No, slightly more than that. Twenty-three, I'd say."

When the baby, a boy, arrived, Hugh said to Stella, "We must ask Andrew to be Edward's godfather."

Stella smiled. "All right. I suppose he'll be pleased. Nobody else will ever ask him to do something like that."

Every year Andrew sent a present to his godson on his birthday. He also wrote a postcard to Hugh every couple of months, in which he said much the same thing every time. "Surviving down here. Hope you're all right. I look forward to seeing you when you're next in town."

One Friday a postcard arrived with a slightly different message. "My dearest friend," it read, "I hope that you're happy in your life. I get along, I suppose. They've invited me to go to work in America—at MIT. I don't think I'll go. I have to stay here, I've decided, for young Edward, and also for you and Stella. So I've told them no. Yours ever, Andrew."

Hugh read it out to Stella. She looked saddened. "Poor Andrew," she said.

"Yes," said Hugh. He felt sad too.

"His *dearest friend*?"

He nodded. "*Only* friend," he said.

Stella thought about this for a few moments. Then she said, "Do you think he's happy?"

"That depends on us," Hugh replied.

Amuse-bouche

LIFE

&

ITS PITFALLS

X-RAY SPECS

George had always wanted X-Ray Specs (as advertised).

He saved up his pocket money and sent off for a pair.

He was very disappointed.

Always read the small print ...

HAROLD HOLLIS, WATER DIVINER

Harold Hollis was a water diviner. He detected the presence of underground water by holding two sticks in front of him.

If the sticks suddenly pointed down, there would be water below and a well could be sunk.

One day Harold's sticks suddenly pointed straight up. "It's going to rain," said Harold.

"I don't need a diviner to tell me that," said his client dismissively.

So ... don't state the obvious, or, if you do, don't expect to be paid for it.

CONCEPTUAL ART

Steve lived next to an art gallery.

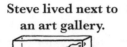

He had an old car.

One morning he discovered a group of people standing around his car. These were Turner Prize judges!

The judges thought it was an installation. Steve's car had won that year's Turner Prize.

With the prize money, Steve bought a new car.

THE SAINTS

The arrival of a new saint in Heaven is always a big event.

"Don't overdo the miracles," the older saints advise.

In the evenings the saints play the guitar and talk about politics.

"Eternity's going to seem awfully long," one new saint said.

So ... not everybody goes marching in.

SCIENTIFIC ETHICS: A CRASH COURSE

A biological scientist working at the cutting edge of fly genetics ...

Discovered that by manipulating a certain gene he could produce monster flies ...

This discovery had commercial implica-tions, especially for waste disposal.

Before After

But he stopped the experiment, burning his papers.

Nuclear scientists did not do this.

TALES

of

MEETING IN LIFTS

MR. NARIMAN SODAWATERWALLA
MEETS LEILA COMMISSARIAT

on the

EIGHTH FLOOR OF THE CRICKET
HOTEL, MUMBAI

Parsi surnames often refer, as many surnames do, to a profession or occupation. In the case of the Parsi communities of India, these followers of ancient Zoroastrianism have traditionally added the suffix *-walla* to occupations to produce a family name that is then handed down through the generations. This practice has produced a slew of colourful surnames, often associated with the role an original family member has played in the production of food. There are people called Cakewalla, for instance, or Bakerywalla, while other names refer simply to the occupation or characteristic without any suffix, as is the case with the surname Commissariat or Papadkhao, a less than complimentary surname meaning *hoarder of poppadoms*. Perhaps the most famous of these occupational surnames is Sodawaterwalla, which was the name of Mr. Nariman Sodawaterwalla, the deputy headmaster of Government Secondary School No. 34 in Mumbai.

One Saturday morning Nariman set out from North Mumbai to visit an aunt of his who had travelled down from Delhi and was spending a few days in the Cricket Hotel near the Wankhede Cricket Ground. This aunt was an ardent cricket fan and was proposing to spend her time in Mumbai watching a match that was being played against a touring Australian side. Nariman was fond of his aunt and made a point of keeping in touch with her, as they were a small family. There were other Sodawaterwallas around, but these were very distant cousins, at best, and probably not related in any meaningful sense. Nariman himself was a bachelor, although at thirty-eight he was certainly still regarded as eligible in the Mumbai Parsi community. He himself felt that it was likely that he would marry, although he would prefer to reach the rank of headmaster before turning his attention to such issues.

Once admitted to the lobby of the Cricket Hotel by the officious guard at the door, Nariman took the lift, pressing what he thought was the button for the tenth floor, where his aunt was staying. In fact, he inadvertently pressed the button for the eighth floor, and it was on that landing that he stepped out, at the same time as did the woman with whom he had found himself sharing the lift. He then made his way towards the second room along the corridor, to the left, having been told by his aunt that this was where she was to be found. That door, though, was the door of the woman from the lift, and they now found themselves standing outside it together, she with the key in her hand.

She looked at him suspiciously, ready to run back towards the lift should his intentions prove disquieting. But Nariman quickly reassured her.

"I'm very sorry," he said. "I must have got out on the

wrong floor. I thought this was the tenth floor. Plainly, I am mistaken."

The woman smiled. She could tell from his diction that he was a respectable, educated man, not one who was intent on robbery. Nobody who was up to no good would say, *Plainly, I am mistaken.*

"It is a mistake easily made," she said. She allowed her gaze to rest on him briefly, on his features, his sympathetic face— a *kind* face, she thought. She glanced at the ring finger out of ancient habit—nothing, and that pleased her, although she reproached herself immediately for thinking of such things—and he a perfect stranger, met in a lift of all places.

"I'm always doing things like that," Nariman said. "I tried to get in the wrong car at school the other day. It looked very much like my car." He noticed her clothing, which was clearly expensive, perhaps even tailored for her rather than bought off the peg. Yes, it had that look about it. And her jewellery, which was discreet but real. In the matrimonial columns of *The Times of India*—which he had to admit he would occasionally sneak a look at, not that he really needed to, being an eligible bachelor and on the lists of every Parsi mother in Mumbai—she would be described as *of well-off family*. There were so many signs for us to read, even in a casual meeting like this—the unwritten biography, he had heard it called.

"All cars look the same," she said. "Although it's not as bad as the old days when there were only those Ambassadors around."

He laughed.

"You're a teacher?" she asked.

He explained that he was, and she said that she worked for an educational supply company and that she was attending a two-day meeting at a nearby conference centre. "It's easier to stay in a hotel at this end of the city for the whole conference rather than to get back to Juhu in the evening."

"Yes," agreed Nariman. "The traffic these days . . . worse and worse." He sighed. *Like everything else,* he thought. *Worse and worse. Poor India: what would Nehru think if, by some miracle, he came back.*

It was at that point that the telephone inside the room started to ring. "I must answer that," she said, "but please, come in. I have a suite. We can continue our conversation."

He went in, finding himself in a large well-furnished sitting room. A door to one side led to the bedroom and bathroom beyond. While she answered the telephone in the bedroom, he looked out of the window over the city's skyline. A large bird flew past, its wings almost touching the window. He watched it drop away and then soar on a thermal current from the hot street below.

"No caller," she said. "Some silly person must have dialled the wrong number."

He introduced himself. "I am Nariman Sodawaterwalla," he said.

She inclined her head. "And I am Leila Commissariat."

They smiled at one another, their Parsi identity having been quickly and unambiguously established by their names.

"Please let me make you coffee," said Leila. "How do you like it?"

It was while they were drinking their coffee that two men let themselves into the room with a purloined pass key. One of them was a photographer, and he rapidly took several flash photographs of Leila and Nariman sitting on the same hotel sofa. There was confused shouting, and then a hurried departure of the men.

"What on earth was that?" asked Nariman.

Leila looked down at her hands. "They will have been sent by my fiancé. I have discovered he is a very suspicious, nasty man, and he has been looking for reasons to cancel our engagement."

"But those men . . . the photographs?" It was the photographs that worried him: Nariman had visions of their production in court, in some sort of breach of promise action, perhaps, and the cloud of shame that would descend on him from that. He would have to resign because one could not have a deputy headmaster being publicly involved in that sort of business.

Her explanation calmed him. "He needs to show evidence to his father," she said, "if he is to avoid being accused of acting dishonourably. Frankly, I am pleased that he will be withdrawing from the arrangement."

Over coffee, she told him the full story of her ill-starred engagement. He listened sympathetically. Over the months that followed, he heard more about that, but also got to know her family, was approved of by her father, and eventually proposed himself. She accepted him graciously.

Leila Commissariat was the daughter of a film producer who made Bollywood epics. Her father took to Nariman

Sodawaterwalla and found him a senior job in his production company. "It is better than being a deputy headmaster," he said to Nariman.

Nariman proved to be an extremely successful producer. Later on, he took to directing and in this new capacity made several award-winning films, including one about a deputy headmaster who becomes a successful underwater photographer and secretary-general of the United Nations.

"Life can become art," said Nariman Sodawaterwalla. "And the other way round, of course: art can become life."

"True," said Leila Commissariat.

WHAT HAPPENED TO PHIL BUTTERS
IN THE LIFT

For seven months, Phil Butters spent almost every evening, Monday to Friday, writing his novel about life in
Wichita between 1958 and 1963. He spoke to few friends
about this, the only people who knew of this manuscript
being his wife, Holly, and his college friend, Charlie van der
Horst. Phil was an osteopath, as was Charlie. They went
bowling together once a month while their wives spent the
evening in a quilting circle of which they were members.

"Phil, when are they going to be releasing that book of
yours?" asked Charlie.

"Not so fast, Charlie; I have to finish it first," Phil replied.
"Then I have to find a publisher. Not easy, you know."

"They'll be falling over themselves to publish it," Charlie enthused. "It'll be on the best-seller lists, I reckon. Sure
to be."

"It's good of you to say that, Charlie," said Phil. "But I
don't know if it'll be that simple. You have to get an agent
first. Publishers won't read anything unless it comes through
an agent."

"You don't say!" Charlie exclaimed.

"So that's the first thing I've got to do," Phil continued. "I
have to get an agent in New York. That's where they are, you
know. Step number one."

"They'll be fighting over you," said Charlie. "And what's it called, this novel of yours? Have you chosen a title yet?"

"I was thinking of calling it *Wichita People*," replied Phil.

Charlie thought for a few moments. Then he nodded and said, "Great title. *Wichita People*. Yep, lots of human interest there."

Phil finished his manuscript a few months later. He had made several copies of it, and these he sent, together with a synopsis, to four literary agencies in New York. After a few anxious weeks of waiting, he called each of these in turn to enquire as to whether they had reached a decision on representing him. In each case the person at the other end of the line revealed that if he had sent the manuscript without a preliminary letter it would be treated as an unsolicited submission and discarded.

"I didn't know the form," Phil said.

"Well you do now," said one of the agents, "but frankly, the climate for your sort of book is, well, hardly encouraging. It's a novel, you say? What did you call it? *Kansas People*?"

Phil corrected him patiently. "*Wichita People*."

"There's not much call for that sort of thing, you know. We'd be wasting your time if . . ."

He barely heard the rest. How could anybody write off another's work just like that, calling it *that sort of thing*. How could he possibly tell?

"But what if I'd written a new *Peyton Place*? And you passed up on it just because it's set in Kansas?"

"But you haven't written a new *Peyton Place*, have you? You've written *Kansas People*."

"*Wichita People*."

"Yes, *Wichita People*. But look here, Mr. . . ."

"Butters."

"Yes, you see, Mr. Butter . . ."

"Butters."

"You see, everybody thinks they can write a novel. Everybody. And it's not easy to place even the most accomplished writers—it really isn't. I can't just get on the phone to an editor down at Random House and say there's a guy out in Kansas who's written this book, you see, and he says it takes the lid off what happens out there. I can't do that, you know, because he wouldn't stay on the line. I'm sorry to be so blunt, Mr. . . ."

"Butters."

"Yes, I'm sorry to be so blunt, but I just don't think so. Sorry."

Increasingly discouraged, Phil approached another two agents with a synopsis and received courteous but brief replies. Nobody was interested. Eventually, despairing of getting anywhere with agents, he made an appointment with an editorial consultant in New York. He would take the manuscript to him personally and discuss what might be done. If necessary, he would pay the consultant to edit it in such a way that it might have a chance of acceptance by an agent.

The offices of the Script Prepare Editorial Consultancy were on the tenth floor of a building on the Upper West Side, two floors above the offices of a well-known publishing house. On the morning of his pre-arranged appointment, Phil entered the lift in the lobby. The door was just about to close behind him when a man joined him in the lift. As the doors closed, this man inadvertently bumped into Phil, causing his briefcase to open and spill the contents on the floor. That was *Wichita People*, and it now cascaded down, all four hundred pages of the typescript.

The man was extremely apologetic. Crouching down, he began to pick up the disordered pages to hand them back to Phil. But then he glanced at one of them, stood up, and began to read it.

He looked up guiltily. "Sorry," he said. 'It's just that my eye fell on the opening paragraph there. Great stuff."

"It's my novel," said Phil.

The man looked down at the page once more. He read a few more sentences. He looked up. "You wrote this? You did?"

Phil nodded.

"But it's great," said the man. "I think this is really great. This is going to hit all the lists."

"I wish a publisher would say that," said Phil wistfully.

"But I am a publisher," said the man.

Amuse-bouche

GEOFF'S CAT, STANLEY

GEOFF'S CAT'S STRATEGY

Geoff's cat, Stanley, was too lazy to chase mice …

But he had learned something from a Russian cat …

He destabilised the mice …

Fake Cheddar

And got them to chase themselves.

So … be careful of outside intervention.

EXPERIMENTAL METHOD

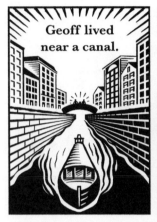

GEOFF'S CAT, STANLEY, SEES THE VET

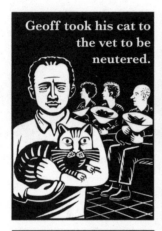

GEOFF'S CAT, STANLEY, MEETS COUSIN AL

Cats have a way of going up to people they know don't like them.

Geoff's cousin, Al, came to stay. Al was allergic to cats. Geoff's cat, Stanley, made a beeline for him.

This is Al in the guest room at night.

This is Al at the table.

Al was quite relieved when he went home the next day.

Unreciprocated love is often poignant.

TALES

of

REVENGE

ON THE WAY DOWN

O n her fortieth birthday, Janice discovered that her husband, Eric, a successful couturier, was having an affair
with a particularly empty-headed model called Marlene,
known by some, unkindly, as *la Vacuum*. "It might not have
been so bad," she confided in her friend Alice, "had I discovered it on a *normal* day—if you can call any day normal
these days. It *might* have been different. But on your *fortieth*
birthday who doesn't feel a bit vulnerable? I'm only human,
after all."

Alice was sympathetic. "I know exactly how you must feel,"
she said. "And with *la Vacuum* as well, with her *tiny* head!" She
looked at Janice discreetly; she had allowed herself to put on
far too much weight, she thought. *Avoirdupois* was no ally of
romance.

Janice did not confront Eric, but seethed inside. She had
seen Marlene at several of her husband's shows, and now,
in retrospect, she remembered intercepting an exchange of
glances between them. The eyes of a lover are drawn to the
object of affection in a particular way; it is not something that
can be easily disguised.

She moved through anger, raw and biting, to a state of
bleak, unfathomable despair. It was easy for Eric—he had
so much: his career, his circle of friends in the fashion industry, his looks. Having given up her job years before, she had

very little, really, and she simply could not face the thought of starting over again.

Her mood darkened. Alice did her best to cheer her up, pointing to the way in which she herself had made something of her life after her own husband had given her up in favour of golf, but Janice seemed beyond the reach of any encouragement.

I'm going to throw myself out of the window, she said to herself. *And it will all be his fault.* The possibility that Eric might feel guilty appealed to her. *He deserves to suffer*, she thought.

They lived on the third floor of an expensive apartment block, Danube Mansions. On a Monday morning, filled with a sense of hopelessness, Janice opened one of the windows, climbed onto the sill, and with her eyes firmly closed, threw herself out into space. On the way down she heard birdsong—a sudden trill of sound. She felt regret: the world was a place of beauty and enchantment, and yet she had not noticed it. She opened her eyes and saw first the sky, and then her husband.

Eric had come home to retrieve his passport for a trip he was planning to make to Milan. He was directly below the window when Janice jumped out. She landed on him. She survived. He did not. He left her the *haute couture* house. One of her first acts as *directrice* was to fire Marlene. "I know you have difficulty reading plain English," she wrote to her, "so to help you I shall use big letters (what *we* call capitals): YOU'RE FIRED!"

Life improved thereafter, and a few months later she went on holiday with Alice, to Venice, where they both stayed at the Gritti Palace and drank negronis.

CLARENCE MACPHAIL

Clarence Macphail was an actor who never really made it on the stage itself. He had been a success at drama school, where he had been nominated for, although not awarded, the accolade *The man most likely to play Hamlet.* That might have come true: after graduation, he was taken on by a travelling Shakespeare company, but was given only very small parts, including that of a tree in *Macbeth.* Disillusioned, he left the Shakespeare company and auditioned for the part of the gentleman caller in *The Glass Menagerie.* That was his first, and last, major role in the theatre. After that, theatrical work dried up, and from that point he turned to television.

At first, that proved to be not much more successful. He was given parts in various productions, but they were usually very small ones, sometimes with no lines to say. In police dramas he might be the man in the white forensic suit investigating the crime scenes; on one or two occasions he was the body itself—usually a sign that an actor is not going to go very far in the industry.

"I am not much more than an extra," he complained to his friends.

"Keep at it, Clarence," they said. "You never know."

Then Clarence was cast in a leading role in a long-running soap opera. This was bread-and-butter work for an actor—exactly the sort of job that people liked because of its regularity. If you played your cards right, you could end up with years of steady work, appearing on screens virtually every day in the case of the more popular dramas.

"It may not be Hamlet," Clarence said. "But it pays the bills. And I'm beginning to get a bit of face recognition. The other day somebody stopped me at the railway station and asked me if I was who she thought I was."

"And were you?" his friend enquired.

"I'm not sure," said Clarence. "Possibly, but the train drew in to the platform and she boarded it. But it was definitely face recognition."

After Clarence had been acting in the soap opera for two years, he was now widely recognised by those who watched daytime soaps—not that they got out very much. He was enjoying the life, which was not too demanding and which allowed him two days off a week to take on small jobs recording advertisements. Those were hardly challenging, but paid remarkably well. That was a help with the mortgage that Clarence had taken on to buy a small detached house with a red roof and a lean-to garage on the side.

Then the company that made the soap opera appointed a new director. She was a woman called Marcia Posthwaite, and after she had been working on the soap opera for three weeks she made an unambiguous pass at Clarence. "You can come and rehearse your lines at my place this evening," she said. "I'll make dinner."

Clarence held her gaze. He was in no doubt as to what she intended. He did not want to go. He had been seeing Annie Macpherson, a viola player, for several months, and he had no interest in Marcia. He wanted Annie Macpherson to come and live with him in the house with the red roof, and he thought that there was a good chance that she would. The lean-to garage, he said, could be converted into a studio in which she could practise her viola. Now he had to deal tactfully with Marcia's invitation.

"Do you mind if I don't," he said, as politely as he could.

Marcia turned away. No man had ever turned her down—certainly no young actor with an interest in his career. She said nothing.

The next day, at the script conference, it was revealed that the character played by Clarence was to be written out of the story.

"I'm afraid you're going to be run over by a tractor," Marcia said, avoiding Clarence's eyes. "Sorry about that. We'll make the episode later today."

Clarence was friendly with the head cameraman, Bill Gillman, who was a distant cousin of his. Bill said, "I've got an idea, Clarence. Leave it to me."

Together they shot the episode in which Clarence was disposed of. Then, when Marcia had left the set, they shot an entirely different episode, in which Clarence proposes to the show's heroine, and is accepted. This new episode also featured an unfortunate sudden end for Vince, one of the other characters, who was a cousin of Marcia's and who had been given the role on that basis. Vince did not appear, of course, but the news of his demise was passed on to Clarence on screen.

Then Bill handed this new episode to the station manager, with instructions that it was to be transmitted that evening in place of what had already been planned.

"New plot development," he explained. "Marcia's orders."

Marcia was furious when she heard what had happened. "*You're* history," she screamed at Clarence.

"Correction," said Clarence. "You're history, Marcia. Bill has been filming you secretly. He has a record of everything you've been up to."

This was not true, and Clarence had no idea of Marcia's misdeeds. But it worked. She gasped, and paled.

"You can always resign," said Clarence. "There'll be no scandal that way."

She did. Bill applied for the job of director, and got it; he was, after all, Clarence's cousin. He then created a role for his brother, Freddy, whose wife was related to Clarence's viola-playing girlfriend, Annie Macpherson.

"Soaps are complicated," said Annie. "All those relationships."

"Just like life," said Clarence.

Amuse-bouche

LIFE

&

ITS FURTHER PITFALLS

CITIZEN'S ARREST EXPLAINED

If you see somebody committing a crime, you are entitled to arrest him. This is what the law says.

Charlie Williams (24) arrested a bank robber.

At the resulting award ceremony, Charlie tried to arrest the mayor for corruption.

He (Charlie) is now under arrest.

Never exceed your powers.

CULINARY MINIMALISM

A chef by the name of Roberto Tagliafferi was famous for his minimalism. He wrote successful books about how to cut things out ...

Those on a salt-free diet turned to his works. The same applied to those who wanted to cut out sugar.

His dishes became smaller and smaller – stripped of sauces and the like ...

And his most successful work involved recipes that called only for olives ...

And yet, people asked, how come he's so fat?

CARGO CULT

On a remote island in the South Pacific the locals believed that the gods would drop gifts from the sky.

A missionary tried to end this cult. "Heathen nonsense," he said.

At that moment a US Air Force plane dropped a large load of relief supplies.

These landed on the missionary's head.

Remember ... don't engage in cultural imperialism.

THE PUDDING

The poet, W.H. Auden, was notably untidy.

Mrs Stravinsky found a horrible mess in the bathroom. She flushed it down the loo.

Puzzled, Auden said, "I put the chocolate pudding in the bathroom to cool down. Now it's gone."

Mrs Stravinsky looked out of the window.

Don't rearrange your host's arrangements.

CELEBRATING MODEST ACHIEVEMENTS

Edgar Wilson drove all the way from Vancouver to Toronto in 1957.

He had one flat tyre on the journey He changed that himself. That happened just outside Saskatoon.

"Things were a bit flat in Saskatoon," quipped Edgar.

On the journey he consumed eighty-six cups of coffee.

All of this happened before Pierre Trudeau made Canada cool.

TALES

of

SCHOOL LIFE

&

AN EDUCATIONAL ONE

IN THE SWIMMING POOL

Captain Edwards had been in the army. Nobody was quite sure what he had done there; the chemistry teacher, Miss Paterson, said that he had been a member of a special unit that was dropped by air and blew things up behind enemy lines, but this theory was greeted with scorn by Miss Oliver, in charge of history, who said, her voice laden with frank disbelief, "Exactly what lines are we referring to, Miss Paterson?" And when Miss Paterson was unable to be more specific, Miss Oliver gave her own view that because of his interest in horses Captain Edwards had obviously been a cavalry officer. To which Miss Salad, the French teacher, had retorted, "How very interesting, bearing in mind that we don't have cavalry any longer," adding, "as you may have noticed." It would, of course, have been simple for one of them to have asked him directly about his army career, but there was something about his manner that discouraged such a direct approach. "He's far too handsome to *pin down*," Miss Paterson once observed, and those to whom she had made the remark knew exactly what she meant.

The school was exclusively for girls, of whom there were three hundred and fifty, many of them being boarders, the daughters of parents who lived abroad or who, for one reason or another, wanted their offspring to be schooled in a pleasant corner of rural Somerset, far away from the distractions of the city, namely boys, cafes, cinemas, and parties. The girls, by and large, were happy at the school, as it was a reasonably liberal institution, which allowed its senior pupils to spend most of each Saturday in the sedate neighbouring town of Bath, where they soon found boys, cafes, cinemas, and parties. The headmistress, Mrs. Grangemouth, was popular with the girls, with the result that, apart from one or two incidents of the sort that are inevitable in any school, there was seldom any problem with discipline. There had been Angela Horder, of course, but most people were beginning to forget about her.

Captain Edwards was not the only male teacher. Mr. Harper, one of the two music teachers, had been there for eleven years, and Mr. Evans, who taught mathematics, had been on the staff slightly longer. Both of these teachers were within sight of their retirement. Mr. Harper planned to be re-engaged on a part-time basis, and Mr. Evans, whose wife was Portuguese, was planning to move to the Algarve. They were both much-appreciated teachers who got better than average academic results. Mr. Harper had established a school wind band that had consistently won prizes in local competitions. He himself was a good jazz trumpeter, although he was now complaining about his embouchure. "That's the trouble with *anno domini* for a wind player," he said. "It catches up."

Captain Edwards had been at the school for eighteen months. He taught some geography to the junior girls, but his principal responsibility was to teach girls how to ride. It was a strong selling-point of the school—and for this reason something prominently featured in the school prospectus—that riding lessons were available to every girl. To this end the school had a stable of eight horses, looked after by Captain Edwards and his assistant, Bobby, a man from the nearby village, who used to be a tractor driver on one of the local farms.

Eighteen months was long enough for Miss Paterson, Miss Oliver, and Miss Salad all to fall in love with Captain Edwards, who was single, although it was rumoured that he had once been engaged to a Danish actress. None of the three teachers ever mentioned to any of their colleagues that she had a romantic interest in Captain Edwards, and he himself was almost certainly unaware of it. Had he been more perceptive, he might have noticed the lingering glances at school meetings, or have wondered why these three teachers were so keen to bring carrots to feed the horses, but as it was he did not seem to be aware of any of this.

For their part, each of the teachers suspected the others of nursing a passion for the dashing and debonair equitation teacher. Miss Paterson, in particular, had seen the way in which Miss Oliver tried to grab the seat next to Captain Edwards at every staff meeting, and Miss Salad had noticed how Miss Paterson was insinuating herself into the teaching of geography so as to be able to stand in for him in the classroom if there was some problem with the horses. "In view of the fact," she said to Miss Oliver, "that she knows *nothing*—and I mean nothing—about maps and such things, it's fairly obvious, to me at least, what her game is. Indeed, I wonder whether she knows where the Nile is, poor woman." She drew breath before continuing, "And how can you teach geography, may I ask, if you are the *slightest* bit hazy about the course of the Nile?" She paused. "I just ask that question— that's all. I just ask."

Miss Salad was perhaps the most desperate of the three. Her problem was that Captain Edwards simply did not notice her. It was not that he was rude in any way—he was most gentlemanly in his manner—but he simply did not seem to see her. She had tried addressing him at a staff party, but he did not appear to hear what she said, and was anyway distracted by Miss Oliver, who offered him a drink—in a rather pushy way, thought Miss Salad. *If only he would talk to me,* thought Miss Salad. *We'd have so much to say to one another—I'm sure about that.* But you couldn't really say very much to somebody who failed to notice that you were there.

It was this desperate yearning that led to Miss Salad's fateful plan. It was not a plan that was worked out well in advance—it was, rather, one of those plans that is hatched on the spur of the moment when the opportunity presents itself. Miss Salad was picking roses in the school rose garden one Saturday afternoon when she saw Captain Edwards riding in the field that ran along one side of the school's heated open-air swimming pool. It suddenly occurred to her that if she were to pick her moment correctly, she could pretend to have fallen into the swimming pool. She was a perfectly competent swimmer, but on this occasion she would be in difficulties and would shout for help—a call that would be answered by Captain Edwards. He would leap into the pool and save her, possibly having to administer mouth-to-mouth resuscitation if she affected to have swallowed water. That was a delicious thought.

Without hesitating to consider the feasibility of this plan, Miss Salad abandoned her roses, darted towards the side of the pool, and launched herself into the water. Breaking to the surface, she cried out, as loudly as she could, and with a certain stylised spluttering, *"Au secours! Au secours!"* The French had not been planned, but she did, after all, teach the language, and that seemed appropriate in the circumstances.

Hearing the calls for help, Captain Edwards immediately cantered across the field to see what was happening. Then, leaping off his horse, he ran the several yards that separated him from the swimming pool and dived headlong into the water to rescue the flailing Miss Salad. *At least he's seen me,* Miss Salad said to herself, adding, *enfin*, at last.

Unfortunately, Captain Edwards had dived into the pool at the shallow end and as a result struck his head on the bottom. This led to a brief concussion, and instead of rising to the surface, he sank. Seeing all this unfold before her, Miss Salad panicked and struck out wildly to the place in the pool where he had disappeared. There she dived down, grabbed hold of one of his arms, and pulled him to the surface. He floated up easily enough, but her grip failed, and he rapidly sank down again.

At this point, Miss Paterson, who had been cycling into the village, saw what was happening and ran as fast as she could to join in the rescue. She was the holder of a life-saving medal and did not hesitate to jump in, reach the scene of the accident with a few quick strokes, and take over the rescue initiated by Miss Salad. In no time she had the captain on the side of the pool, stretched out before her. Following life-saving procedures to the letter, she cleared his chest of water and administered mouth-to-mouth resuscitation. Miss Salad looked on, dripping and shaking, filled with remorse at what she had done.

Captain Edwards responded quickly. "Good heavens," he said, as he came to. "Are you kissing me?"

Miss Paterson laughed, and gave him a real kiss this time. "Mouth-to-mouth," she said. "You'd swallowed a bit of water, I'm afraid."

Captain Edwards smiled, and then kissed her back. Miss Salad watched grimly.

Miss Paterson and Captain Edwards announced their engagement five months later. Miss Salad might have minded—she might have minded terribly—but as it happened she did not. She had met one of the parents, a man who had lost his wife a year or so previously, and although he was a bit older than she was, they had become very fond of one another. "I'm getting engaged as well," she said to Miss Paterson, adding, "as it happens."

Miss Oliver met a market gardener shortly after the engagement of her two colleagues. "I'm going to go and live with him," she announced to Miss Salad. "I shall be giving up teaching and helping Jim with his market garden. Behold, you are looking at a true daughter of the soil!"

"Bonne chance," said Miss Salad.

Overhearing this exchange, Miss Paterson thought: Just like Miss Oliver, Miss Salad could not resist a dig.

BOARDING-SCHOOL STORY

David arrived at his boarding school at the age of thirteen, struggling to suppress the sobbing that had convulsed him in his father's car. That was in 1965. The school was called Eton College.

In the front seat, his mother pursed her lips, staring fixedly at the road ahead. She did not like the idea of boarding school, but had succumbed to her husband's arguments. And now that David was going, she had been obliged to endure this tearfulness in the car, and her husband's grim determination to see the whole thing through.

His father glanced in the rear-view mirror and said, "Come along, David. Look at the positive side of things. You'll make new friends—lots of them. I did. Uncle Johnny, for example, he was a friend of mine at school. Same house. You'll meet plenty of people you like—you really will."

He did not answer his father. If he spoke, he thought it would be in sobs. He did not want to go to boarding school. He wanted to stay at home, in his own room. How could he sleep in a dormitory with a lot of other boys? What if he talked in his sleep? What if . . .

His father was saying something again. "We'll be there soon. You see over there? That building? I can tell you all about that. I remember it very well, you know."

"Did you pack those extra socks?" asked his mother,

desperate to make the abnormal normal. "The ones I put on your dresser? Did you remember them?"

An hour or so later they said goodbye. David tried to smile, but he could not.

"You'll be fine," said his father. "You'll be happy as a sand-boy."

David wondered what a sand-boy was, and why sand-boys were so happy. Presumably they were not sent to boarding school, or they would not be so happy. And he was anything but happy, his misery increasing with each year he spent there. He disliked everything about the place. He disliked the hierarchy and the strutting arrogance of the senior boys, in their plumage. He lived in fear of the punishments that were meted out for minor infringements of a code of conduct that was ill-defined and opaque. He disliked the social disdain that so many of the boys, the off-spring of snobbish parents, manifested in their everyday attitudes. He hated Ancient Greek, which he was made to learn, against his every instinct. What was the point of learning a language that nobody spoke any longer?

At the age of sixteen he decided to run away. He had discussed the matter with a friend in the same house, and they had agreed that they would try to make their way to Ireland. "We can get a job there," said the friend. "I know somebody who's got a cousin with a racing stable. We can help look after the horses."

They absconded one Saturday night, making their way to the local bus station, where they boarded a bus to Liverpool. From there they would have caught the ferry to Dublin had they not been spotted by a policeman. He thought them young to be travelling on their own, and, following on unconvincing answers being given to him, he took them back to the police station. There the true story emerged, and they were fetched by David's father the following morning.

"You should have told me how unhappy you were," he said.

"I tried," said David.

His father was silent. "So, what now? Do you want to go back there?"

David shook his head.

"Don't make him," said his mother.

His father hesitated. "But where will he go if he doesn't go back to Eton?"

His mother had obtained an educational directory from the local library. Her eye had been caught by an advertisement by a school in France that offered tuition in English. "How about France?" she said. "I saw a picture of a place there called St. Bernadette's. It's in the Auvergne. I rather liked the look of it."

They wrote to St. Bernadette's. They were only too happy to offer a place, as their enrolment had dropped dangerously and they needed new students. They did not disclose, in their answer to the letter of enquiry, that they were, in fact, a girls' finishing school.

David went willingly to St. Bernadette's. They made him very welcome, giving him his own room at the back of the main house. There were twenty-two other students, all girls. They were learning French, Kitchen Skills, Flower Arranging, and the History of Fine Art. There were also occasional lessons in deportment and etiquette.

David was very happy. He drank coffee each morning in the nearby village with a small group of the girls from the finishing school. In the evening they played Monopoly and canasta. They went skinny dipping in the river, where the water was cold and clear. He hoped the year would never end.

THE CURE

I was a psychotherapist. That's what I used to be. I did it for twenty years, Monday to Friday, and then suddenly one day I said to myself, "You really shouldn't go on with this." And so I undertook a career change and became the manager of a motorcycle cinder-track circuit. I have four people working for me, and I like my job. Often, when I get up in the morning, I look in my shaving mirror and say, "Wise choice, Bill."

I know, of course, that it's a rather unusual progression. There are very few people in the cinder-track world who are qualified clinical psychologists or psychotherapists. I'm both, as it happens. I started off as a clinical psychologist and then specialised in psychotherapy. I have all the necessary qualifications, and, in addition, I'm a psychoanalyst. That means I've had a proper Freudian training, including a full training analysis. As far as I know, there's nobody else in cinder-track racing who has undergone full analysis, as I did as part of my training. These things take time, and you have to be committed to complete the course.

I started doing general psychotherapy, but after a year or two of treating phobias and various neuroses I began to specialise in children. I had a job with a clinic that took on children who needed therapy. There are always, I'm sorry to say, lots of those, as many children have a rotten start in life and need assistance to get along. Child psychotherapy is good work that helps young people who might otherwise fall by the wayside.

Because of where my practice was, I had referred to me a certain number of rather over-indulged children. These were young people who had been, in old-fashioned language, spoiled. They were given everything they wanted—often by parents who felt guilty because they had given their children so little time. It's easy to think that you can make up for that by showering children with presents—but it never works. What children want is love and attention. That's absolutely basic.

I began to get annoyed with my patients, which was a bad sign. I felt like shaking some of them and saying, *Do you realise how lucky you are? Do you realise what you have when there are so many kids throughout the world who have so little?* But that, of course, was not the way we did it. We had to listen to the young people and then help them to get over their problems by giving them insight. That was the theory—and I went along with all of that for years, and then, rather to my surprise, I became a rebel. I found that I could spend hours with a patient and at the end of the day get nowhere. The spoiled brat continued to be a spoiled brat. The little minx continued to be a little minx.

I had an epiphany, and it was this epiphany that was responsible for my leaving psychotherapy and going into dirt-track management. This is what happened.

An eight-year-old boy was brought along by his mother. He was a late thumb-sucker, and the dentist had said that it was affecting the growth of his teeth. If he continued to suck his thumb, he would need orthodontic work to straighten his front teeth. The family had tried everything: offers of rewards (a bad idea) as well as reasoning (not a particularly strong idea with an eight-year-old). The mother went off and I had the patient to myself.

I said to him, "Now listen, Cedric"—that was what the poor boy was called—"now listen, Cedric, have you ever heard of the Suck-a-thumb Man?"

He looked at me blankly. And so I told him all about the Suck-a-thumb Man, who is a character in a nineteenth-century German children's book called *Der Struwwelpeter*. It's a book that has frightened generations of Germans with its vivid pictures of what happens to bad children. In the case of thumb-suckers, the Suck-a-thumb Man was pictured running after them with a great pair of tailor's scissors to cut their thumbs off. Blood gushes from the stumps of the severed digits. *Der Struwwelpeter* is not exactly a modern favourite.

Cedric listened wide-eyed. "So you'd better be careful," I said. "You'd better stop sucking your thumb, young man."

His mother phoned up a week later. "How on earth did you do it? He hasn't sucked his thumb once since I brought him to you."

"Advanced methods," I said. "Advanced, child-centric methods."

Then there was another patient, a boy of twelve, who had been causing any amount of trouble for more or less everybody. He sat in my room chewing gum with studied insolence. His language was highly offensive, every second word being an obscenity. He had been through the system several times, and nobody could do a thing with him.

I listened to him bad-mouthing his parents. Then I stopped him. "You listen to me," I said. "I'm going to give you one chance, right? One chance. I'm going to be watching you, son. I'm going to be watching you really closely, and if I hear from anybody—from your teachers, from your parents—that you've been giving anybody any lip, any lip at all, I'm going to come after you."

He stopped chewing the gum. His eyes widened.

"Yes," I said, "I have friends, you see, and my friends and I will come round to your place and beat you up. Understand?"

He stared at me, saying nothing. Then I said, "I mean it. I really mean it. So now I want you to get out of here, wait outside for your mother, and when she comes to collect you, you apologise. Full apology for being what you are and all the grief you've caused her. And promise to behave better in the future. And you apologise to the teachers at school. Full written and signed apology. Understand?"

Slowly, he nodded.

Those were two of my successes, but there were many more—all achieved in much the same way. I had founded, it seems, a whole new school of child psychology. But by then I'd had enough. I was the only one using these highly effective methods—everyone else was talking about getting through to children, using reason, and so on. I had no support, in spite of getting such good results, and so I decided to give up. One day, though, I think I'll write a book and tell people where psychotherapy is going wrong. Somebody has to do it. It might as well be me.

Amuse-bouche

CAESAR

&

THE WORLD OF ROME

Julius Caesar, Roman Emperor, had the whole world to invade …

But he always chose to invade Gaul.

GAUL →

He liked the restaurants there, the cuisine …

… and the style. The French were elegant, even by Roman standards.

Dressing well can sometimes bring un-welcome attention.

THE CATS OF ROME

Stanley's Roman ancestors went off to the Coliseum most Saturdays.

The cats liked to watch dogs fighting lions. The dogs always lost.

In the interval, they drank milk and ate fish.

Then they went home.

CAESAR'S DOG

Caesar's dog, Cassius Canis Nobilis, led a charmed life …

He had a personal groom and a personal walker …

and a whole retinue of slave dogs …

But he still had fleas, as flea collars were yet to be invented.

Don't romanticise the past.

THE IDES OF MARCH

Julius Caesar, Roman Emperor, received numerous warnings on all sorts of subjects …

"Beware the Ides of March" was one message he took seriously. He made plans …

Brutus and his friends waylaid Caesar. "Take that, Julius!" said Brutus.

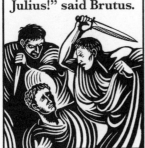

Caesar was ill-prepared. He had thought the Ides of March was the following day …

Always adjust to daylight-saving time.

TALES

of

FRIENDSHIP

FOUR DENTISTS GO ON HOLIDAY

Tom and Marjory had met at dental school, swiftly fallen in love, and married immediately after qualification. They bought a building in a quiet road in a suburb of Glasgow. At first they were alone in the practice, but when the premises next door came unexpectedly onto the market, they were able to knock a dividing wall down and create a suite of additional surgeries. "We're going to be big, Marj," Tom said to Marjory.

They advertised for two extra dentists to join them in their partnership. This advertisement was answered by a Canadian who had practised for twenty years in the Yukon, but who wanted to come and live in Scotland. He was called Macdonald, and along with his letter of application he sent a photograph of himself wearing a kilt. He had a large red beard and wild, staring eyes. They scrutinised the photograph together and burst out laughing. "No, thank you," said Tom, in his slightly camp way of speaking. "He can carry on looking after those *remote* teeth!"

The other application was from another husband and wife team. They were called Janine and Bob. They also came from Glasgow originally, although they had trained elsewhere. "They look ideal," said Marjory.

The two couples soon formed a good working relationship. They also got on well together socially, and at the beginning of that first summer, they decided all to go on holiday together in France. They would drive south in an old Mercedes-Benz that Tom had inherited from an uncle. They would stay in hotels recommended in a guide that Bob had picked up somewhere and that was entitled *France for Dentists*.

They set off. In Beauvais, where they made their first overnight stop, they found a small museum, La Musée des Dents, dedicated to dentistry through the ages. The display claimed that French dentistry had always been far in advance of its equivalent in other countries, especially Britain. "I'm not surprised," said Bob. "The French are far better at so many things than the English, whatever the English claim."

Marjory, who was half English and half Scottish, turned on him. "Are you saying English dentistry is rubbish?"

Bob shook his head. "All that I'm saying is that I shouldn't be surprised if French dentistry is better even than Scottish dentistry."

"We have nothing to be proud of," Tom interjected. "I mean, nothing to be proud of in Scotland. We can't point the finger at the English. Look at the appalling state of teeth in Glasgow over the years. Remember those mouth clearances that people had in their early twenties? All that sugar?"

Janine felt that she had to defend Glasgow teeth. "It's much better now," she said. "I agree: it used to be bad, but it's better now—it really is. Even in places like Drumchapel. You actually see some teeth there these days—you never used to."

Bob looked askance at her. "Jan, it never was that bad. And Edinburgh wasn't all that great when it came to dental hygiene. They were hypocritical."

"Who's hypocritical?" Tom challenged. "Are you saying Edinburgh people are hypocrites? Is that what you're saying?"

Bob was placatory. "No, I wasn't running Edinburgh down. It's just that Edinburgh can have a bit of an attitude problem sometimes."

"Let's not argue," said Marjory. "Look at this display here. Look at that extractor! What a beautiful old instrument."

They dined that night at a restaurant called Le Chanson de Roland. They all had game paté for their first course, followed by halibut prepared with *beurre blanc*. Tom and Marjory chose to have cheese rather than dessert, but Bob and Janine ordered a double helping of crème caramel.

"You shouldn't be eating that," muttered Tom. "Those desserts are loaded with sugar. Think of what they're doing to your teeth."

Bob put down the spoon with which he had started to tackle the brittle crust of the pudding. "Excuse me," he said. "My teeth are my affair. And if I want to eat crème caramel, I don't think I need your permission."

Tom met his stare. "I take it that you advise your patients to avoid sugar. I assume that you do."

"Of course he does," snapped Janine.

"It's just as well, then," Tom said, "that none of his patients can see him now."

Marjory tried to lower the temperature of the exchange. "I'm so looking forward to tomorrow," she said brightly. "I love being in France. Such a beautiful country, and with this delicious cuisine . . ." Her gaze drifted to the crème caramel, and then quickly drifted away again.

The next day, in a small country hotel called l'Auberge de la Truite, they had a heated disagreement over root-canal treatment. That was followed, in a restaurant in a small town near Montpellier, by an acrimonious argument over the replacement of mercury fillings.

"I think we should go on holiday separately in future," Tom said to Marjory that night as they prepared for bed. "I like Bob and Janine, but . . ."

"No need to say more," said Marjory.

HARRY BRICK

There was a doctor called Andrea who was a vociferous opponent of male violence in any form. "Men are very violent creatures," she said with a shudder. "And by men, I don't mean *people*—I mean males. Do I need to spell it out: men are brutes." And she spelled it out carefully, lingering on each letter: "B R U T E S."

A friend said to her once, "Andrea, you should go to a boxing match one day. It'll disgust you. Men hitting one another. It's horrible, but you need to see it in order to understand just how awful men are."

"Oh, I know that," said Andrea. "Boy, don't I know that!"

"But you should still go," said the friend. "Every so often we need to have these things confirmed, you know."

With some reluctance, Andrea followed this advice and bought a ticket for a big boxing match that was to be held in a neighbouring town. The highlight of this occasion was to be a match between Harry Brick and Martin Slugger. Both of them brutes, thought Andrea as she studied the programme.

She sat in her ringside seat, horrified by what she saw. Brick hit Slugger, and Slugger hit Brick. The crowd loved it, and cheered when Brick was knocked to the ground. The umpire bent down to examine the felled pugilist and stopped the match, as Brick had a cut above his eye.

The regular doctor was ill, and so there was an appeal for

one. Andrea answered this when nobody else stepped forward. She was taken into Brick's dressing room, where she attended to the cut above his eye. That took no more than a few minutes, but it was long enough for her to fall in love with him. These things may seem unlikely, but they do happen.

She took Brick out for dinner, and they started to see one another. Her friends, of course, were concerned.

"This Brick character you're seeing," said a male colleague. "I'm not convinced he's the right man for you, Andrea. I think you need to think about it."

Andrea ignored this advice. People in love often ignore the advice of well-meaning friends. Then, a few weeks later, that same colleague saw Andrea and Harry Brick in a coffeehouse. This colleague said, "Oh, so here's your famous pugilist."

This did not go down well with Brick. He was not sure of the meaning of the word *pugilist*, but he did not like it. Rising to his feet, he threw a punch that connected fairly and squarely with the colleague's chin. Down he went, not unconscious, but nonetheless convincingly felled.

Andrea looked at Harry Brick. She was now not so sure that the relationship was going to work out after all. And in that she was right: they saw one another once or twice afterwards, but the gap between them was too great.

She subsequently married a cosmetic surgeon called Carter, whom she had met while she was on holiday in Florida. He was a sensitive man with a soothing manner, and they were extremely happy. Harry Brick continued to box, but gave it up when he married Joan, a lay minister in the Methodist Church. Joan taught him that boxing was wrong, and that men should be more in touch with their feminine side. "Jesus will help you do this," she promised.

Harry helped Joan with the small florist's shop she ran. One day, who should come into the florist's shop to buy roses for his wife's birthday but Martin Slugger! Harry felt a sudden, disturbing urge to hit out at Slugger, to settle ancient scores from the boxing ring, but conquered this by closing his eyes and humming Joan's favourite hymn, "Guide me, O thou great Redeemer."

Harry opened his eyes. He saw red. But it was only the red of the roses that Martin had chosen for his wife.

"She'll love those, Martin, old pal," said Harry.

Amuse-bouche

MORE CATS

STANLEY'S DNA

Geoff was interested in DNA. He sent off for a DNA testing kit.

The kit had a swab. Geoff decided to find out about Stanley's origins? Siberia? The distant plains of Africa?

"It's interesting to know where you come from," Geoff said to Stanley.

The results arrived – complete with Stanley's genealogical chart:

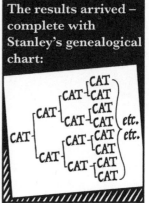

GEOFF'S CAT, STANLEY, AND HIS FILM CAREER

The producers of *Lassie, the Wonder Dog* were to make a film about a Wonder Cat.

Action!

DISMAY

GLOOM

After the audition, the producer spoke to the owners.

"Film's cancelled," he said. "Casting difficulties."

Some films never get made.

GEOFF'S LAZY CAT, STANLEY

Geoff's cat, Stanley, was extremely lazy. Even purring was too much of an effort for him …

Geoff happened to see a gym for cats. "That's the place for Stanley," he thought.

'Buff Cat' Gym

Open 24 hours

But Stanley just slept on the cross trainer, and on the rowing machine …

The gym refused a refund. "None of the cats who come here do anything," said the director.

GEOFF'S CAT, STANLEY, SEES A PSYCHIATRIST

It is well known that cats, like humans, can suffer from psychiatric conditions ...

Geoff took his cat, Stanley, to see a veterinary psychiatrist ...

The psychiatrist tried free association. He showed Stanley a picture of a mouse: no reaction.

"We can do little for cats," said the psychiatrist. "Dogs, yes; cats, no."

TALES

of

STRANGENESS

AT THE ARACHNOPHOBIA WORKSHOP

Robert was afraid of spiders. He feared and hated them with a passion, and, as far as he could ascertain, spiders were able to detect this hostility, and repaid it in full measure. When Robert encountered a spider, it would glare at him before unambiguously advancing in a purposeful and aggressive fashion, ready to attack. This usually induced in Robert a sense of overwhelming dread.

"You misinterpret spiders," said Robert's girlfriend, Jenny. "They're just doing their thing. It's not their fault they exist, for heaven's sake!"

"I just hate them," Robert replied. "I hate the way they look. I hate their way of walking sideways. I hate everything about them."

Jenny looked reproachful. "Hate is corrosive, you know."

"I don't care. I didn't start this business with spiders, they did."

"No, Robert, that's nonsense. Spiders have never done anything to you. Have you been bitten? No, you haven't."

"They'd bite me if they had the chance."

Jenny laughed. "They're tiny. Imagine how big you look to them. No, you need to do something about this." She paused as she remembered something. "Have you thought about going to an arachnophobia workshop? I've just seen one advertised. They're free. I think they're run by people who are interested in spiders, who actually like them, and who don't like the idea of people persecuting them." She paused again. She usually managed to get Robert to do the things she wanted him to do. "You should go, Robert. You've really got issues here, you know—you should go."

So Robert went to the workshop, which was held in a local community centre and was attended by ten people.

"All right," said the workshop leader, a thin man named Terence. "Hands up if you have issues with spiders."

Ten hands shot up.

"No surprises there," said Terence. "Okay, people; time to deal with these issues!"

Robert winced. He was not ready. You have to be ready to deal with issues before you try anything. There is no point in dealing with issues prematurely—or so he had been taught at another workshop he had attended. That was called "Dealing with Your Issues," and he had found it moderately helpful, although clearly some issues remained. "Nobody gets rid of their issues altogether," said the leader of that workshop. "We all have what we call *residual issues*."

But now Terence was explaining to the group how he intended to proceed. "I shall use a technique known as flooding," he said. "Psychotherapists use it when dealing with phobias. It involves exposing the patient to the very thing that is feared. In this case . . ."

Robert—and several others—gave an involuntary shudder.

"In this case," continued Terence, "it means introducing you to this friendly little creature here."

And with that he reached into his pocket and took out a small box. Opening this box, he took out a large brown spider.

The spider hopped up onto the palm of Terence's hand and stared at him with what appeared to be a dozen pairs of eyes.

Robert gasped. How could anybody even think of doing such a thing?

"See," said Terence calmly. "This little chap is perfectly harmless. He's interested in what's going on—that's all. And so I'm going to put him on the table so that you people can take a good look at him and get to know him."

Robert closed his eyes. He felt his heart thumping. The back of his neck was unusually warm.

"Adrenaline," muttered the woman next to him, gripping the edge of the table so tightly that her knuckles showed white.

"Oh Jesus, Mary, and Joseph," whispered a man on the other side of the table. "Protect us."

"Now," said Terence. "While you're looking at our friendly visitor, I'm going to write his name on the board. He has a Latin name and a common name. I'll give you both."

He turned to face the blackboard at the end of the room and began to write the spider's names in chalk. His back was turned. He did not see what was happening. There was a resounding thump.

Terence turned around again to face the class. Now it was his turn to gasp as he looked at the table.

"Who did that?" he barked.

The spider was in the middle of the table—quite squashed, a pile of disassembled protein. Small spider legs lay at impossible angles, some detached, some still joined to the rest of the carcass.

"Who did that?" repeated Terence, his voice rising. "I am very, very disappointed."

Nobody spoke, but they all looked relieved.

"You're not going to own up, are you?" said Terence.

"No," said Robert. "We're not." The woman next to him had relaxed her grip on the table and was breathing normally again. The man who had invoked the protection of the Holy Family was crossing himself with relief. He looked at the others. Everybody in the workshop—with the exception of Terence—was in full agreement. And at that point, Robert had a moment of insight. What so often—and so tragically—unites human beings, he thought, is fear. But then he thought: Hope can do the same thing, can't it?

He rose to his feet. "I tried," he said to Terence.

The others followed his lead and stood up too. Everybody was leaving.

Jenny asked him after he came home, "How did it go?"

Robert replied, "Well, we looked at a spider and . . ."

"And?"

"Actually the session ended earlier than anticipated."

"But you made progress?"

Robert hesitated. "I wouldn't exactly call it that."

ENLISTMENT

I'm going for a run," said Gordon to his wife, Ellen. "The usual route."

They were staying in a villa in Corsica. This was on a hill; a short distance down below was a sprawling barracks of the French Foreign Legion, la Légion Etrangère. Gordon had pointed it out to Ellen. "That's the Foreign Legion, believe it or not," he said. "*Beau Geste* and all that. They wear *képis* and those funny khaki aprons."

She had looked at the gate and the buildings beyond. Everything had that familiar, sparse look of army bases any-where in the world. Neatness. Order. Toughness. She hated all of it—it was so alien. Men created such emotional deserts when they were left to their own devices.

"Anybody can join," he said. "You turn up and they'll take you as long as you aren't wanted by the police for murder. Can you believe it? That's the only restriction. They'll give you a false name—*un nom de guerre*. Then you disappear."

She spotted a guard standing by the barrier and shuddered. "Awful," she said. "Just imagine."

"Mercenaries," said Gordon. "That's what they are."

Now, on his run, Gordon found himself making his way along the perimeter fence of the barracks. He stopped to catch his breath—he was not as fit as he had been—and it was while he was standing there that a military vehicle came tear-ing towards him on the dusty roadway.

"You!" shouted a man in uniform. "Yes, you! Name? Unit?"

Gordon stood stock-still. As the vehicle drew to a halt he tried to explain himself. He spoke good French and thought he was making a good job of the explanation when he felt himself being seized by two legionnaires and being manhandled into the vehicle.

He was brought before the commandant. "Dubois?" snapped the officer. "Jean Dubois?"

Gordon shook his head. "I'm a visitor," he said.

The commandant laughed. "Aren't we all?" he snapped. "Thirty days. Desertion. And consider yourself lucky. In wartime I could have you shot."

He was taken to the prison block in the middle of the camp. There he was given military fatigues and a metal bowl into which a glutinous green soup had been poured. He banged on the door, demanding to see a lawyer, but this request was greeted with laughter.

He heard nothing from his wife. She had reported him to the police as missing, and there had been a widespread search. This had produced no results.

At the end of his sentence, Gordon was taken back to a barrack hut and given a uniform. He would be sent the following day, he was told, to a French military base in Chad, in West Africa. "If you serve conscientiously," a colonel told him, "then you can get French citizenship after five years. Imagine that! A Frenchman in five years!"

Gordon shook his head. "There's been a terrible mistake," he said. "I never signed up."

The colonel looked at him with bemusement. "Do you think I volunteered?" he asked.

Five years later, Gordon was given home leave. He returned to Scotland, where he had lived, to find that Ellen had had him declared dead by the courts. She had married a personal financial adviser and was living in Aberdeen in a house with a small infinity pool. When Gordon reappeared she said, "I'm coming back to you, Gordon."

The financial adviser was understanding. "You can just see how these things happen," he said. He contacted a former girlfriend from his student days, and, after an annulment of the marriage to Ellen, married her. Then they bought a caravan park in Portugal and left Scotland to live there.

Gordon and Ellen returned to their previous life. "No more holidays in France," said Gordon.

'No," agreed Ellen. "Certainly not."

He looked at her fondly. "I'm very fortunate," he said. "How many wives would forgive their husband for volunteering for the Foreign Legion for five years?"

She stared at him. "Volunteering?" she asked.

"A slip of the tongue," he said quickly.

LORD LUCAN, FUGITIVE

L ord Lucan was called Lucky Lucan by his friends. He was a very grand man—an earl, in fact, which is not quite as grand as a duke or a marquess, but is not too bad by any standards. He was also a gambler and, by common consent, a man with little to recommend him.

Lord Lucan's main distinction in this life was to have murdered his children's nanny by mistake, instead of his wife. This he did in the basement of his house in a fashionable part of London, lurking in the kitchen as a woman's footsteps drew nearer. He was full of anger, and he laid about his victim with a lead pipe, only to discover that he had killed the nanny by mistake. Shortly afterwards, the countess appeared on the scene and saw what her husband had done. He set about her too, but she fought him off. He fled.

Nobody is quite sure exactly what happened over the hours that followed. The day afterwards, though, Lord Lucan's car was discovered abandoned in a ferry port, and it was widely believed that he had boarded a boat to France, later jumping overboard in the middle of the English Channel. His disappearance was the subject of great interest and spawned numerous theories and, indeed, frequent sightings of the missing earl in far-flung parts. Lord Lucan was reported to be in a remote corner of Africa (Botswana), in India (Goa), and in New Zealand. If he did survive, and if these sightings had any substance to them, then he would appear to have been extremely peripatetic.

The predominant view was that he was dead, and that in jumping off the ferry he had committed suicide. Eventually, over forty years later, the English courts declared him dead, and for legal purposes Lord Lucan was no more. However . . .

He did drive to Newhaven, in East Sussex. He did get out of his car. He did consider boarding the ferry and fleeing the country, but then he stopped. He thought of what he would miss. He would miss his friends. He would miss the clubs where he played backgammon. He would miss St. James's and his shirt-maker in Jermyn Street. He would miss the Cavalry and Guards Club on Pall Mall. There was none of that in France, and his French, such as it was, would not get him far. He would have to become an anonymous agricultural worker—one of those people who picked grapes down in Bordeaux, or who trampled the vintage with their purple feet. He would have to herd goats in the Auvergne, perhaps, or, if he were lucky, deliver bread from a mobile *boulangerie* in Marseilles. None of these was a suitable occupation for an earl.

So Lord Lucan decided to stay in England. And no sooner had he made this decision than there occurred to him a brilliant idea. He would evade capture *by pretending to be Lord Lucan*. Like all brilliant ideas, this one was quite simple. He would wait a few weeks for the immediate fuss to die down, and then he would return to London. Once there, he would go to the Cavalry and Guards Club, announce at the porter's desk that he was Lord Lucan, and say that he had come to collect his umbrella, left behind in *the toilet*. That would be the exact term he would use: *the toilet*. Now, Lord Lucan knew, of course, that *nobody* from that stratum of society used the word *toilet*. They said *lavatory*. And so the porter—who understood these shibboleths—would immediately think, "This man is an imposter—he's clearly not a real earl." He would call the police, and Lord Lucan would be escorted to the street outside. "Yes, yes," the policeman would say, "so you're Lord Lucan. And while I accept there is a certain likeness, my answer to you is that I'm the archbishop of Canterbury. Now on your way, sir, and don't be bothering these gentlemen again."

Word would get round, though, and soon everybody would have heard that there was a Lord Lucan look-alike who was claiming to be Lucky Lucan. "Of course, nobody's fooled," they would say. "He gives himself away, you'll understand. He says quite the wrong thing."

This widespread belief that there was a bogus Lord Lucan about would mean that the real Lord Lucan would be able to live in London once again with complete impunity. And that is exactly what he did, taking up residence in a modest flat in Mile End and getting a job entertaining people in a busy Soho pub with his Lord Lucan impressions. The locals in the pub loved that, as did the management, who put up a notice saying, *See Lord Lucan here tonight for £2.50*. "He's just like old Lucky Lucan," said the pub's denizens. "You know—the geezer what did in that poor girl instead of his missus. Him. Dead ringer. Very funny."

A film director visited the pub. He was making a film about the disappearance of Lord Lucan, and he had heard that there was a very skilled Lord Lucan impersonator who might be suitable for the role. He found the missing earl playing backgammon with a couple of builders in the pub and invited him to have a quiet word outside. There he made the offer of the role of Lord Lucan in his forthcoming film, for which he would pay a fee of eighty-seven thousand pounds and one per cent of any profits. Lord Lucan accepted with alacrity. "I can talk posh when required," he assured the director. "You'd think I was the real thing."

The director smiled. "You don't fool me," he said. "But I'm not the target audience. You'll fool them easily enough."

The shooting of the film went well.

"You're a really good Lord Lucan," said the director.

Lord Lucan acknowledged the compliment with a nod of his head. "It comes naturally," he said. "I don't really have to act."

The final scene was shot on a ferry to France, specially hired for the film. The director explained to Lord Lucan that he would be filmed climbing onto the railing and then jumping into the sea. "We've rigged a net," he said. "It won't be in the shot—it'll be just below the railings. You'll look as if you're falling into the brine, but you won't be."

Lord Lucan nodded. He would practise the jump into the net, once they were out at sea.

They set off. The film crew was having dinner when Lord Lucan went out on deck to smoke a Balkan Sobranie cheroot. He sauntered over to the railing. *I'll have a quick practice jump,* he said to himself.

He jumped. He was on the wrong side of the ship. There was no net. Lord Lucan was not all that bright.

Down below, the members of the film crew were enjoying their dinner of fish and chips, washed down with warm beer.

"Where's the talent?" one of the cameramen asked.

"Having a smoke up on deck," said the make-up artist.

The water was cold. It was dark. It embraced Lord Lucan, took him down.

The following morning, after the entire crew had carried out a fruitless search of the ship from bow to stern, the make-up artist said to the best-boy (electric), "There's a certain justice, isn't there, in the way things work out? Not always, of course, but sometimes."

The best-boy agreed. "Fancy a peppermint?" he said.

LITTLE PIGGISH

The opera house was more or less in the centre of the city, and the city was more or less in the centre of Germany. It had been built in the mid nineteenth century, designed by an architect who was subsequently charged with offences that required him to spend the rest of his life in exile in France. Its style was Baroque, with elaborate boxes and a great deal of gilt. People travelled considerable distances purely for the pleasure of sitting on its red plush seating under a soaring painted ceiling. The opera company for which it provided a home was well regarded, even if not in the first rank. It was, singers advised, a good place to start, but not necessarily the best place to end up.

The doorman in this opera house was a very short man called Little Piggish. His job was to supervise the stage door, where he had a small office. In the office there was a register for recording the arrival of stage hands as well as singers and members of the orchestra. He wore a blue uniform with narrow gold bands on the epaulettes. Piggish was proud of that uniform, which he said was based on that worn by Prussian cavalrymen of the eighteenth century. Nobody believed that, and it was widely thought that Piggish's uniform had been designed for him by his aunt, who owned a Wall of Death in a nearby town's amusement park.

Piggish lived as a lodger in a house owned by a Polish couple, Mr. and Mrs. Kowalski. Mr. Kowalski had been a clock repairer but had been obliged to give this up when his hands were badly affected by rheumatoid arthritis. Mrs. Kowalski made hats. They let their spare room to Little Piggish, who had lived with them for eleven years.

"Have you ever thought of marrying?" Mrs. Kowalski asked Little Piggish one day. "You'd be a good catch for some lady, you know."

Little Piggish was pleased with this compliment. "That's kind of you to say that, Frau Kowalski, and who knows? Perhaps one day. We'll see."

The truth of the matter was that Little Piggish had been smitten by an opera singer, the soprano Anya Bistedral. Anya, who was locally known for her portrayal of Mimi from *La Bohème*, was widely appreciated in that part of Germany. She could have taken up roles much further afield, but she preferred to stay where she was because she looked after an elderly mother close by, and she did not like the idea of travelling off to Munich and Berlin, let alone Milan or New York.

Little Piggish worshipped Anya Bistedral. She barely noticed him, though, although she always greeted him politely when she arrived for performances. "Oh, good evening, Herr Piggish," she would say as she swept past his cubicle.

He would leap to his feet, but by the time he was standing, Anya Bistedral would have disappeared into her dressing room. The dressing room was always full of flowers, placed there by Little Piggish. He received bouquets of flowers from admirers of Anya Bistedral, taking them in from the men who called at the stage door asking to see her. He always turned these men away—handsome, tall men—telling them that

Anya Bistedral was receiving no callers. He would, he said, pass on their flowers, along with the cards that accompanied them. Once the caller had gone, though, Little Piggish would extract the cards, tear them up, and then put the flowers in Anya's dressing room, sometimes with a card from himself saying, "I hope you like these flowers! Hans Piggish."

He sat in his cubicle and thought of Anya Bistedral. He imagined himself playing the male lead opposite her. He imagined singing one of the great love duets with Anya. As he sat there, he heard the applause from the auditorium as Anya Bistedral reached the end of a great aria. He imagined what it would be like to be onstage with her, receiving the applause. And then they would withdraw to the wings and go off for dinner together in the *fin-de-siècle* restaurant next to the opera house.

One evening a gentleman caller who had been pursuing Anya Bistedral for some time managed to get to her dressing room during the interval by a route that did not take him past Little Piggish's office. The singer listened to his invitation to dinner with a severe expression on her face and then sent him packing. Leaving the opera house at the end of the show, she stopped at Little Piggish's cubicle.

"I had a very tiresome caller this evening, Herr Piggish," she said.

Little Piggish sympathised. "I do my best to keep them away, Frau Bistedral," he said. "I really do."

Anya Bistedral looked at Little Piggish and smiled. She was tired of being pursued by men. She needed somebody reliable, somebody who would be no trouble. It suddenly occurred to her that Little Piggish would be a very comfortable husband for somebody: small, unobtrusive, and, most importantly, undemanding.

She smiled at Little Piggish. "You wouldn't care for a bite of dinner tonight, would you?" she asked. "If you happen to be free, that is."

Anya Bistedral and Little Piggish married six months later. Anya's elderly mother died shortly before the wedding and so they started their married life in her flat. Then Little Piggish's aunt, the one who owned the Wall of Death motorcycle ring, invited them to take over her business, as she felt it was time for her to retire. Anya Bistedral decided that she needed a rest from singing, and so she and Little Piggish went to live in a large caravan parked next to the Wall of Death at the fairground. They were very happy.

Little Piggish learned how to ride a motorcycle on the Wall of Death. He proved to be very popular with the crowds. In due course he taught Anya Bistedral how to ride, and she took to it very readily. Sometimes she would ride and sing Wagner at the same time, which always brought the house down.

Brought the house down . . . Some things we do can bring the house down. Love, kindness, acts of generosity to those who have little in their lives, a hand on the shoulder, a look, a considerate word. These things can bring the house down.

MORE HEARTWARMING STORIES OF LOVE

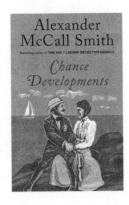

Chance Developments: Stories

Inspired by vintage photographs, these five lyrical stories capture the surprising intersections of love and friendship that alter life's journeys.

Emma: A Modern Retelling

Jane Austen's classic novel as retold in the twenty-first century—carriages have been replaced by Mini Coopers and cups of tea by cappuccinos, but Alexander McCall Smith's sparkling satire and cozy sensibility are the perfect match for Jane Austen's beloved tale.

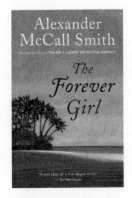

The Forever Girl

In a close-knit community of expats on Grand Cayman Island, a mother and daughter try to navigate their lives, as they are torn between dreams of love and the reality they face.

La's Orchestra Saves the World

A moving novel about the life-affirming powers of music and loving companionship during a time of war.

My Italian Bulldozer

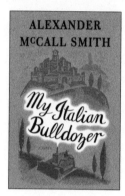

A delightful romp through the lush sights and flavors of the Tuscan countryside. *My Italian Bulldozer* is a charming and intensely satisfying love story for anyone who has ever dreamed of a fresh start.

Trains and Lovers

A wonderful novel that explores the nature of love—and trains—through a series of intertwined romantic tales told by four strangers who meet as they travel by rail from Edinburgh to London.

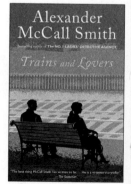